DAYS AMONG THE DEAD

Alan Trevithick is released from prison when fresh evidence clears him of the murder of Milo Hagerty. He owes his freedom to Dorothy Merrack, his cousin and childhood sweetheart . . . Her discovery of the real killer puts Alan's life in jeopardy. A second murder leads them behind the scenes at a crematorium, and finally to the Spanish monastery of Montserrat. Alan Trevithick finds a new twist in the quotation 'My days among the dead are passed.'

Books by Ivon Baker
in the Linford Mystery Library:

THE BLOOD ON MY SLEEVE

IVON BAKER

DAYS AMONG THE DEAD

Complete and Unabridged

LINFORD
Leicester

First published in Great Britain by
Robert Hale Limited
London

First Linford Edition
published 2006
by arrangement with
Robert Hale Limited
London

British Library CIP Data

Baker, Ivon, *1928* –
   Days among the dead.—Large print ed.—
Linford mystery library
   1. Detective and mystery stories
   2. Large type books
   I. Title
   823.9'14 [F]

ISBN 1–84617–257–8

Published by
F. A. Thorpe (Publishing)
Anstey, Leicestershire

Set by Words & Graphics Ltd.
Anstey, Leicestershire
Printed and bound in Great Britain by
T. J. International Ltd., Padstow, Cornwall

This book is printed on acid-free paper

1

The night they abolished hanging I dined with the prison governor. His wife had been watching TV in another room, and fanned through our cigar smoke with tidings of how the Lords Spiritual and Temporal had voted. We pondered the news in silence.

After a couple of minutes the chaplain cleared his throat, and I braced myself for another platitude. It came.

'You really have a lot to be thankful for,' he fluted, blinking in my direction.

I shrugged my shoulders. 'Gratitude comes hard after eighteen months in this place.'

Even then he could not leave well alone. 'I'm sure we all know just how you must feel,' he chirruped.

The governor noticed the glint in my eye. 'More whisky?' he asked softly. I forced a smile and held out my glass. No point in parading my bitterness.

Tom Boulting, the fourth member of the party, eased upright in his armchair. 'I, for one, haven't the faintest idea how you feel,' he muttered in the rasping croak which puts the fear of God into opposing counsel's witnesses. 'But I know this: you're the classic argument for abolition.'

Tom had defended at my trial, and this was his long-delayed hour of triumph. In spite of his brilliance, I had been convicted, and successive appeals, right through to the C.C.A., had proved useless. Now I was free again. Two years after the murder for which I had been sentenced, fresh evidence had substantiated the alibi on which I had always insisted. I knew what Tom meant. If the death penalty had not been in abeyance, that fresh evidence would have meant posthumous exoneration — a hollow victory. Yet I could not agree with him. As I sat there, watching the curling smoke of my cigar, I considered even death preferable to the degradation I had endured. And it could have been thirty years . . .

I gazed up at the ceiling and listened

while the others talked.

'Can you sue for wrongful arrest?' asked the chaplain. I sensed that they were all looking in my direction, but I left that one to Tom Boulting.

'Can't say anything about that, Padre,' he rasped. 'There's a deuce of a lot of sorting out to be done.'

'The Sunday papers will be after the story,' said the governor quietly.

Again, Tom acted as advocate. 'Could be. I'm not sure, though. Where's the story?'

'Where's the story?' spluttered the chaplain. 'Good gracious, it's a *marvellous* story. I can just see the headlines. ALAN TREVITHICK FREED. INNOCENT MAN'S TWO YEARS . . . ' He hesitated.

' . . . of hell,' I said, without looking at him.

He coughed. 'I wasn't exactly going to say that,' he murmured reproachfully. 'After all, life here isn't really all that bad. Now you must admit that.'

'I've learned not to admit anything.'

'Oh, but I hope you're not going to be uncharitable. I'm sure that when you come to look back . . . '

I let him ramble on. *Look back*. On what? A continuing process of depersonalisation. Throughout the whole time I had been regarded as a killer. Even worse, from my point of view, my conviction had branded me a liar. Ten men and two women had listened to all I said in my defence and had then dismissed it as a pack of lies. Over a period of twelve months no less than five learned judges had endorsed their opinion. That rankled. And I remembered so well the governor's words when I continued to protest my innocence even after the rejection of my final appeal. '*Of course, Trevithick, I realise you have to say that. But it's all rather pointless, don't you think? Far better to accept what's happened and try to settle down here. With your background, we'd be glad of your help in the library. Once you've proved that we can rely on you!*'

Now he was in an awkward position. He could hardly say, 'I knew you were innocent all the time.' Yet the situation demanded something more than the customary handshake and pat on the shoulder as I made for the gate. The dinner that evening was the best he could do by way of gesture. Ironically, it only served to deepen my bitterness. The meal itself was mediocre — the governor was no gourmet and his wife was obviously grateful for that. Yet the courses had been served in order and we had used real plates and the appropriate cutlery. Too long had I been one of a queue of muttering men who shuffled to the servery, each grasping a moulded steel tray into which the whole meal was ladled. Then would come the race to reach a table before the stew or the custard made the tray too hot to hold. The oft-repeated quip of the duty officer, *'Get your feet in the trough!'* was too near the truth to be funny.

Look back, my reverend friend? Yes — I could look back to the day I heard that my wife would not visit me again and would not be around when I was released. I wasn't even allowed to digest that news in privacy. The governor summoned me to his sanctum and handed me the letter he had already studied in detail. '*I think you'd better have this straight away, Trevithick.*' And before I had been back in my cell ten minutes, the chaplain was hot-footing it along the corridor to bring me the benefit of his consolation.

Laura believed me innocent of the murder, but could not accept my association with Susan Mordant. Susan, busy on a novel about the Spanish Armada, came often to the museum where I was curator — to check historical details. Her literary style needed checking too. Pedantic — with the resilience of cement. Five years' lecturing had taught me how to bring history to life, and I was happy to share my expertise with Susan.

That novel was her great secret. Hugo, her husband, could have helped far more than I, but she was determined that he must know nothing of the venture until it appeared in print. I knew how she felt. Hugo Mordant wrote bestsellers and could be insufferably patronising.

So I kept Susan's secret — even from Laura. I didn't mention her frequent visits to my office. And there were other visits. I had a makeshift apartment on the top floor of the museum where I entertained the occasional archeologist, or bedded down myself if work kept me late. That often happened after I'd persuaded the trustees to back my plans for a quick-fire series of popular exhibitions.

Susan would ring me at some inconvenient time — when I was experimenting with dramatic lighting effects or rehearsing a *tableau-vivani* — and what more natural than that I should ask her to come round and talk things over when the museum had closed for the night? It became quite a habit, and — hand on my heart — all completely innocent. But *secret* — and that's what made the whole thing look so suspicious when Laura found out. To make matters worse, Laura only learned the truth at the same time as fifty million other people. That was after Susan turned up in my apartment at half past nine one night and found the body. Laura could forgive me the body, but she could not take the idea of Susan being in my rooms at half past nine at night. Incidentally (and it seemed surprisingly incidental after two years of reflection), the body was that of Milo Hagerty. To me, Hagerty was a useful information-man. Several times he had put me on to a valuable chunk of antiquity before it reached the open market. He saved the museum something like ten thousand pounds — and I always paid him a fair commission for his work. Unfortunately, after his untimely demise the police revealed the shadier side of his character. He was a professional smuggler of art treasures who also dabbled in blackmail. When you realise that this blackmailing art-smuggler, in whose favour I had written cheques to the tune of a thousand pounds, was shot with a gun which bore my fingerprints — you may be inclined to sympathise with the jury which doubted my defence.

You can't keep a good murder quiet, so all England and Laura Trevithick learned that the wife of Hugo Mordant had found the late Milo Hagerty in my bedroom.

After Laura wrote to say goodbye, I

wallowed in self-pity and recrimination — but even that luxury was snatched from me. Within a week the chaplain was scratching at the door again, pregnant with evil tidings. My wife had been killed in a street accident. I found myself recalling the good times we had known together — and that didn't exactly help matters.

★　★　★

The governor was speaking.

'If I know the Press, they'll be round the gate in hordes tomorrow morning. D'you want to meet them?'

I thought for a moment. 'It's inevitable, sooner or later. But I'd rather it were later.'

'Fair enough. We'll arrange something. Shall you be going straight home?'

'Home?' I could not keep the mockery out of my voice. 'My house has been shut up for a year. It'll be like visiting a mausoleum.'

'Oh, come now . . . ' The chaplain had to put his professional spoke in. 'You have a whole new life waiting for you out there. This is no time to be morbid.'

Tom Boulting stubbed out his cigar. 'Whatever you decide to do, I'll need your address,' he croaked. 'And so will the police.'

'The police?' I hadn't expected that.

'Naturally. If you're innocent, someone else is guilty. The whole case is opened up again. You'll have the pleasure of renewing acquaintance with Inspector Quill.'

'Pleasure indeed,' I said — and meant it. I bore Quill no malice. He had done the best he could with the evidence available, yet throughout the whole investigation and the subsequent trial I had a sneaking suspicion that he was not entirely satisfied. I had not forgotten what he said before I was taken to court. '*Understand this, Mr Trevithick. I'm not the judge. I'm only a witness.*' He had sounded almost apologetic. Yes, I liked Quill. The prospect of another encounter with him was the brightest spot in the immediate future.

'The point is,' said the governor, 'I've been asked to arrange for you to be taken wherever you want to go. Just say the word.'

I made up my mind. 'Soho. The Countdown Club.'

The chaplain sighed, but Tom Boulting nodded approvingly.

'She'll be there,' he said.

★　★　★

London's night-life holds no attraction for me, so none of my illusions was shattered by the anaemic appearance of the Countdown Club at half past eleven in the morning. Some brave soul had drawn back the heavy velvet curtains and the cold December sun was straining through the grime on the windows. All it touched was turned to dross. The shabby white lacquer on the piano was crazed and chipped; the quilted plastic on the music-stands had been patched with Sellotape, and a heavily-built woman was grimly brushing at a patch of sawdust on the faded carpet where a customer had vomited the night before. Blotches and stains, like a pattern of Aegean islands

11

seen from the air, revealed that the accident was by no means unique.

At the door a dissipated bruiser with a sat-on face had barred my way until I mentioned my name.

'Ar,' he mumbled toothlessly, 'I seen yer pitcher on telly. Come to pay yer respecks to Miss Bowman?'

I nodded.

'That's the ticket,' he said with a leer of approval. 'Once a gentleman, always a gentleman, eh? Froo that door and up the stairs.'

Once through the quilted door, all pretence of opulence vanished. The stairs were uncarpeted and there were no shades on the electric lights. I climbed slowly, held back by last-minute apprehension. At the top of the stairs was a green-painted door bearing a placard which proclaimed the premises beyond as the registered offices of half a dozen obscure enterprises. Each company apparently specialised in 'promotions' — whatever that might mean — and the placard had been defaced by uncomplimentary comments scribbled, presumably, by dissatisfied clients. I hesitated before ringing the bell. Beyond that door was the woman I had come to see — Brenda Bowman. I owed her my freedom, for she had provided the evidence which had cleared me. Brenda Bowman was only her professional name. She had been baptized Dorothy — Dorothy Merrack — and she was my cousin. I had not seen her for twenty years, and the prospect of reunion created a conflict of emotions in my mind.

We had spent most summer holidays together as children, exploring the Costa Brava in the days before it became a tour-operator's paradise. We were there when the location shots for *Pandora and the Flying Dutchman* were filmed. Next time that one comes round on TV you'll see what the place was like when we knew it, back in the late forties.

The childhood idyll ended for Dorothy when her father was killed in Korea. Spain saw her no more — and for a time my summers were lonely. While I was waiting to go up to Oxford I heard that she had made her stage debut. '*But not the legitimate theatre,'* clucked my mother, disapprovingly. My father had been more forthright — and nearer the mark. '*Back row of the chorus, by all accounts. At least she's had the decency not to use her family name.'*

To me it all sounded wildly exciting and I envied her the courage to strike out on her own. I promised myself a visit to the revue in which she was appearing, but the promise remained unfulfilled. Subsequent rumours that she had become a fan-dancer of some notoriety distressed me. It seemed a far cry from our unselfconscious nude bathing in remote Catalonian coves.

And now twenty years had passed and I was afraid of what I would find on the other side of that green door. Would show business have coarsened her? Or was the boot on the other foot now? Had the past two years left a mark which could diminish me in her eyes?

My fears were groundless. She ran across the room to greet me with all the warmth she had shown whenever I arrived at the villa in those far-off summers.

14

'Alan!' She stood on tiptoe to kiss me on the cheek, then stepped back to look at me closely. The appraisal was mutual. In place of the overblown tart I had feared to meet, there was a maturer version of the carefree and beautiful girl I had once known. We were the same age, yet she looked ten years younger. But . . . something was different. There was a brittleness about her; a defensiveness that told of hard blows taken and bitter disappointments lived down. In that moment deep called to deep within us. We were two of a kind.

The important thing was that we had not become strangers to each other. We could talk as freely as ever — and talk we did, to some purpose.

'Thirsting for revenge?' she asked as she busied herself with the coffee percolator.

'I might be — if I knew where to direct my attention. But first things first. I want to say thank you for digging up that photograph.'

'Forget it. I'm only sorry I was so late. It must have been hell for you. Want

15

to talk about it?'

'I'd rather hear your part of the story. It's still a bit of a muddle for me. Everything has happened so quickly.'

'You can say that again. My little party piece acted like the old Open Sesame. And we only got back from Australia a month ago.'

'That was how you missed hearing about the trial?'

'That's right. We've had two years of globe-trotting, but as soon as we got back I slipped down to see Mummy and she told me what had happened. That's when I remembered the photo.'

'Tell me about it.'

She handed me a cup of coffee and settled down beside me on a studio couch.

'On the night of the murder you were in Leeds. You'd been there in the afternoon — and half a dozen people could vouch for that, but no one backed you up when you said you were there until half past eight. Not even the waiters at the hotel where you had dinner. Not that that surprised me.

16

They're a dozy lot.'

'And you were there — while I was having dinner.'

She finished her coffee quickly and put down her cup. 'Two tables away. Amazing, wasn't it? And we didn't see each other. That's not surprising, though. We were having a farewell party, and the other tables could have been empty for all we cared.'

I laughed. 'And I had my nose stuck in a sale catalogue. I seem to remember feeling strong disapproval of your crowd. Especially when that chap took the flashlight picture.'

'And that's the picture which puts you in the clear, Alan. You were just in range of the flash — and I recognised you as soon as I saw the print. Lucky for you I mentioned it to the girls. When the police questioned them last month they remembered how I'd boasted about my brilliant cousin. The police checked *everything*. They didn't just take my word — they ransacked that photographer's place until they found the negative, then double-checked to see if it was a fake. God! They were thorough. If only I'd spotted you sooner. I didn't see the print until we were in New York.'

'I thought you said Australia.'

She grinned ruefully. 'That was only the last bit — and, believe me, we got there the hard way. America first — East Coast, West Coast. You name it; we've been there. Then Japan. Then Down Under.'

'Successful?'

She shot me a quick glance, as though suspecting sarcasm. 'With our show? You must be joking.'

I got back to my business. 'You say you recognised me. But you hadn't seen me since I was a kid. And don't tell me I haven't changed in twenty years.'

'I'd seen your picture in the papers once or twice. And I watched those museum programmes you did on TV four or five years back. After all, you *were* my favourite cousin, Alan. Still are, as a matter of fact.'

'Thanks.'

She patted my hand. 'Don't mention it.' Suddenly she was serious. 'Alan, I'm sorry about . . . about Laura.'

I couldn't be sure how much she knew. I stared at my cup. 'At least she didn't suffer. It was instantaneous.'

'That wasn't quite what I meant,' she said quietly. So, she had heard.

'Let's forget it,' I said, shortly.

'O.K.' She stood up quickly and looked down at me.

'Who done it?'

'Eh?'

'The murder. Who's favourite in your book? Somebody at the museum?'

I had asked myself that question a thousand times, but it was no more than a futile mental exercise. Still, for what it was worth I told her what I considered the only reasonable theory.

Milo Hagerty was a wrong 'un. Looking back, I realise how dim I must have been not to see that. But plenty of other people had realised it, to their cost. Any one of his blackmail victims could have been the murderer. The police had argued that the killer must have known that Milo would be at the museum that night. That let me out, but Inspector

Quill did not believe me when I told him that Milo's visit was unexpected. He usually arrived unannounced, bursting with news of some new treasure about to be sold.

His killer might have been trailing him for days. It could have been pure chance that when he finally ran his quarry to earth it was in my apartment.

At the trial a great fuss had been made about the weapon, but I had my own ideas about that. It was the latest addition to our collection of firearms, and as I had cleaned it and placed it in its showcase myself it was not surprising that the police found my prints on it. When they discovered it, the gun was back in its showcase. The clip was empty, but it had been fired recently, and when they tested it the markings on their specimen bullet matched those on the three they dug out of Milo's carcase. Poor Milo had been a sad case of overkill.

Counsel for the prosecution argued that I had used the gun and then replaced it in the showcase, hoping that it would be like Edgar Allan Poe's purloined letter, undetected in its letter-rack. Apparently the idea was that the police would not suspect me of using a weapon and then replacing it so ostentatiously under their noses. I admit that seemed rather clever. To be honest, it was far too clever for me.

My own theory was much simpler. The gun was not uncommon, and I reckoned that the killer had a similar type in his pocket when he came to the museum. The commissionaire reported that Milo Hagerty arrived an hour before closing time and was shown up to my apartment. He was *persona grata* with us, and I had given orders months before that if he arrived during my absence he was to be allowed into my rooms. I was expected from Leeds by eight o'clock — and would have been back by then if I hadn't just missed the early train.

So if Milo was being followed, it was reasonable to suppose that his killer was in the museum for an hour before the doors were closed for the night. During that time he must have seen the gun — a duplicate of his own — and, maybe on the spur of the moment, decided to use

21

our exhibition model instead. That would spare him the risk of having his weapon traced — and by replacing the gun after the killing he had no need to dispose of his own. We were not particularly security-conscious, I'm afraid, so he could have dodged the attendants on their final round of the premises. The showcase presented no problems. We didn't go in for concealed alarm systems or electronic gadgetry, so he could have picked the lock with a paper-clip. And — just to make his day for him — the gun was in perfect working order — as Milo was to discover at nine o'clock, the time the surgeon estimated he breathed his last.

I had often told Milo to make himself at home — and that was just what he did. After helping himself to my whisky, he had gone into my bedroom, taken off his jacket and shoes, loosened his tie and crawled under the eiderdown to sleep off the exertions of the day. He died sleeping.

In my simplicity I should have said that no man in his right mind would commit murder on his own premises and then leave the body around for the first casual dropper-in to discover. Tom Boulting made that point well at the trial. Surely, he argued, if I had killed Milo, the sensible thing would be to shift his body somewhere else. To leave him there on my bed was to invite suspicion. But it appears that murderers are a subtle breed. The prosecution pounced on that point and tore it to shreds. It seemed that I had craftily banked on the police assuming that such damning evidence must, in fact, be clear proof of my innocence. To me, that argument was so much double-think. But it convinced the jury. They knew all about people like me — so they brought in their verdict and toddled off home to watch *Z Cars*.

Dorothy listened to my tale in silence.

'So you see,' I concluded, 'it could have been *anyone*. God knows how many poor devils wanted Milo out of the way. The police have reopened the case, but they'll never find him. The trail is two years old.'

She was frowning. 'Your idea's reasonable,' she said. 'But it's . . . I don't know . . . a bit too *clever*. Why bother to put that gun back again? Why not just chuck it down on the floor. You admit yourself that there was nothing to link it with the murderer. It's too *clever*,' she repeated. 'Like something in a book. I always think detective stories are too good to be true. I suppose that's why people read 'em.'

We talked of other things after that. The old days in Spain and what we had each been doing since. As I left she said, 'I'm going to check over all the old records of your case. It fascinates me. If I get a brainwave, I'll give you a ring.'

I did not hear from her again for three months.

2

All of a sudden I had money. I had been prepared to sue right and left to get some sort of compensation, but there was no need. Consciences in high places must have been sorely troubled, to judge from the cheques that rolled in. I sold my story to a Sunday paper for what seemed to me a massive figure. Interest in the case revived and I expected a visit from Inspector Quill any day — but the weeks passed and he did not come. My house at Oxted went onto the market, and I set myself up in a service flat in Baker Street, a mere pistol-shot from the site of 221B.

The museum would have taken me back. I don't say they exactly grovelled, but it came near to that at times, and I could foresee embarrassment all round if I accepted their offer. They could hardly sack my successor, but the trustees had concocted a new appointment — Field Director. It sounded fine — and the pay was worth picking up — but I would have been a dogsbody, answerable to trustees and curator alike. Milo Hagerty would have jumped at the job. I turned it down, haggled for a retainer as External Adviser on Roman Antiquities, reminded them that the Bechstein Bequest could stand the extra strain — and left the museum assured of another thousand a year. I could live in idleness until I found what I needed — a job both demanding and irresistible. I wasn't ready for settling down. Soul-destroying routine had governed my life for the past eighteen months. I wanted the taste of it out of my mouth.

Flying out to Madrid to spend Navidad with friends whetted my appetite for travel. In February I was on Spanish soil again, bringing myself up to date with the museum scene in Barcelona.

Back at home I traded my tired Rover for a flamboyant black and gold Capri with a power-bulge down its bonnet — a projectile which would have seemed hopelessly out of character two years before. Grudgingly I had to admit the truth of the prison chaplain's words. A new life was beginning for me.

In March I did the grand tour of Roman Britain, renewing acquaintance with curators and archaeologists. All very enjoyable, but rather pointless — until I hit on the idea of writing a book. I was standing on Hadrian's Wall when inspiration came. Gazing northwards on that blustery March day, I saw myself as a centurion of the Spanish Legion, aching for the sun while condemned to pacify the British and keep the Picts at bay.

The more I thought of that Roman soldier, the more real he became — and that was how the plot for my book was born. My biggest problem was how to tell his story in the style people want to read today. I needed help and advice. Then I remembered Hugo Mordant. Patronising he might be, but he had been a good friend in the past, and I knew for a fact that he had done his best to get Laura to think straight when she had got herself steamed up about Susan and me. Hugo had accepted the truth about those secret meetings, and he urged my wife to do the same. Unfortunately, Laura regarded him as just another arty type condoning his wife's immorality. Still, he had tried, and I was grateful for his efforts. That alone gave me an excuse to visit him. I could mention my book casually and learn something from his reactions. Hugo could be most helpful when he thought he wasn't being asked for advice.

I drove up to Meden Market in response to his invitation. The Mordants had a large Regency house on the outskirts of the village, and I enjoyed a long weekend in their company. Meden Market stands on the edge of the Dukeries and was once within the confines of Sherwood Forest. I was not surprised to learn that Susan — hopeful as ever — was working on a novel set in the time of the legendary Robin Hood. She read a chapter to us, and as I sat watching her I could see Hugo shaking his head sadly in the background. He had good reason. Her work was couched in the style of Sir Walter Scott — full of medieval oaths and ill-starred essays into Authorised Version English. All the knights were 'gaily caparisoned' and every outlaw a 'merry Saxon rogue'. It was all delightfully quaint, but only a publisher of satire would have considered it.

When Hugo and I were alone, I broached the subject of modern literature — not that the subject remained unbroached for long in that house. He spoke with the Olympian confidence engendered by years of success.

'Everyone's chasing *style* nowadays. It's a rat-race for struggling authors. They all try so desperately to be different — and end up doing cheap imitations of Graham Greene or Hemingway. Mind you — it's not exactly easy for me. I'm lumbered with the style I hammered out ten years ago. My publisher won't hear of anything different — and he's got to be right. Anyone can write a book — but it takes a clever man to sell one.'

I gazed out of the window at the distant view of the parish church.

'What are the chances for an author at the bottom of the ladder these days?'

He chuckled. 'Meaning Susan?'

'No, Hugo. I was thinking of myself. I'd

like to tackle an historical novel.'

'Well I'll be damned! You've caught that bug from my wife. O.K. Go ahead. Have a bash — but I can't hold out much hope. Anyway, why history?'

'It's my subject.'

'Of course. Silly of me. But I should have thought you'd have done better to write about your — er — recent experiences. By the way, did you do any of that thing in the *Sunday Whatsitsname?* Or was it all ghosted?'

'Ghosted, I'm afraid. I still think I could have done better myself.'

He laughed and began to fill an expensive pipe. 'Well, you've got self-confidence, anyway. That's in your favour. Mind you, it might be best to keep off crime stories. People expect the plots to be a damn sight too clever these days. It taxes the ingenuity.'

His words struck a chord in my memory.

'Funny you should say that. I have a theory about Milo Hagerty's murder which might make the grade as a novel. My cousin thinks it's clever enough for modern taste — by which she means it's too clever for real life.'

'Tell me more.' He sounded really interested.

When I had finished, he said, 'I like it. I like it. Were you serious about turning it into a novel?'

'Not really. Like to borrow the idea?'

He tapped the stem of his pipe against his teeth. 'It's certainly worth putting in my plot-book. I keep a sort of register of likely plots. It's an insurance for my declining years when inspiration wanes.'

'But do you think it's too clever to be possible?'

He shook his head slowly. 'It's possible — but improbable.'

'So you think my theory's wrong.'

'I didn't say that. I said it was improbable — but that doesn't bother me. Murder is always improbable. That's why it's so rare, thank God.'

We began to discuss my Roman centurion idea. He didn't hold out much hope, but all his suggestions were valuable. I was determined to try my luck.

Before I returned to London, Susan

took me for a long walk round the village. It was Sunday afternoon and the church bells were ringing for early Evensong. Across the road from the church stood the vast Queen Anne Vicarage. As we passed, a tall figure in a cassock was striding down the long drive.

'It must cost him a packet to run that rambling old place,' I said.

Susan followed my gaze. 'It's not quite as bad as it seems. Part of the Vicarage has been converted into a sort of maisonette. That's where Russell Minty lives.'

Her tones suggested that I should know about Russell Minty.

'The artist,' she explained when I made no comment. 'He's turned one of the rooms into a studio. Surely you've heard of him. He's made quite a name for himself, the last couple of years.'

'No comment,' I said — and she had the grace to look abashed.

'Sorry. I forgot. Were you really completely out of touch?'

'Let's say I wasn't encouraged to be a dilettante.'

We climbed a stile and skirted the Vicarage garden. From that angle I could see the front door of the maisonette — a graciously proportioned entrance. Russell Minty was better placed than most artists of my acquaintance.

'What's he like?' I asked. 'All abstracts and collage work?'

'Not at all.' Susan sounded indignant. 'It just so happens that he's doing my portrait — only don't tell Hugo. It's going to be his birthday present, and I want it to be a surprise.'

'How can you keep a thing like that secret? Surely you have to sit for Minty. Doesn't Hugo wonder where you are?'

She grinned impishly. 'He doesn't know. He's away a lot these days, so I only go for my sittings when he's not at home.'

I stood still and faced her. 'Susan — is that wise? Remember what happened the last time you tried to keep one of your artistic ventures secret from Hugo. If Laura had lived she would have been all set to cite you in the divorce court. Is Minty married?'

'No. So there's no chance of a jealous wife making trouble. I'm sorry, Alan, I wasn't meaning Laura specially. And Hugo would never get any wrong ideas. He has his failings, but a suspicious nature isn't one of them.'

Her obtuseness exasperated me. There she was, in a small village, blithely behaving as though she and Hugo were still living in Chelsea. What of local gossip? A married woman who regularly slipped out to spend hours with a single man — and an *artist* at that — as soon as her husband's back was turned. What more could any scandalmonger ask for? And sooner or later, Hugo would hear some distorted version of the story. What price his trusting nature then? And if he did become suspicious, he might well revise his opinion of what went on when Susan was with me at the museum.

But when I spelled all this out to her, she simply laughed and told me not to be Victorian. I left Meden Market with a sense of uneasiness.

★ ★ ★

Back in Baker Street (and how Victorian *that* sounds!), I found that Dorothy had called during the weekend and left a note with the hall porter asking me to call her.

As soon as I heard her voice on the phone I knew she was excited about something. She claimed to have a new line on Milo's murder, but refused to discuss it without seeing me. I suggested dinner, but she told me to talk sense and remember that she worked at night. We settled for lunch at my apartment next day.

I can't say I spent the hours trying to guess what she might have to tell. The life and death of Milo Hagerty had become matter of little more than academic interest to me. Instead, I settled down to work out some action for my centurion.

She arrived prepared for a working lunch. My heart sank within me at the sight of the old newspapers she had dredged up from somewhere. I remembered them all too well. The glib headlines, the blurred photos of Laura and myself, the meaningless exterior shots of the museum, and, of course, the only available likeness of Milo Hagerty.

That picture fascinated Dorothy. She had a sense of the dramatic and led up to her revelation gradually — her fan-dancer's training coming out, I suppose. Her first pertinent remark certainly roused my interest.

'What if I were to tell you everybody in this case has been looking in the wrong direction?'

I regarded her critically. There was a feminine smugness in her tone which warned me not to risk any flippant comment. She must have good reason for that enigmatic question, and, in any case, I was sure she would not drag my attention back to that wretched episode just for the fun of playing detective.

'What do you know?' I asked bluntly.

She gave me a Mona Lisa smile — and that was the moment I realised how lovely she was. Until then I had only seen her as a maturer edition of the companion I had once known.

'Tell me,' she said, ignoring my question. 'Why do you think the solving of this murder is going to prove hopeless?'

'You know why. Because there are so many suspects, and unless Milo kept a register of the people he was squeezing for money we have no idea where to look for any one of them. He covered his tracks pretty effectively.'

'And *that*,' she said, prodding my chest lightly, 'is what I mean by looking in the wrong direction. I don't think the killer was a blackmail victim. *I don't think he even knew Milo Hagerty from Adam.* Tell me something. Did you see the body?'

'No. But I saw photographs.'

'Taken in your bedroom?'

I nodded.

'Tell me how he looked.'

That seemed a gruesome request, but she obviously thought it important. I did my best to remember.

'He was in bed. Well — not exactly *in*, but it looked that way. If it hadn't been for the stains on the eiderdown you'd have thought he was asleep. He'd rolled in on top of the blankets and pulled the eiderdown up round his ears . . . '

She interrupted me. 'That's what I wanted to hear. Now I'm sure I'm right.

Look — ' She fumbled among the newspapers and held one out to me. 'Who's that?' she asked, stabbing a finger at one of the pictures.

'Milo, of course. It says so underneath.'

'Ah, but watch. The celebrated transformation act . . . ' She grabbed another paper and held it against the photograph, covering the lower part of Milo's face. '*Voilà!* Who is it now?'

I frowned and squinted at the picture. 'What am I supposed to say?'

'Oh, for heaven's sake! Can't you *see*? It's *you*!'

'Me?' I must have sounded as stupid as I felt. 'Look, Dot, I know you're on to something — but I just don't get it. Let's have it one step at a time, eh?'

She flashed a sympathetic grin at me. 'Sorry, Alan. That wasn't fair of me. O.K., let's take it from the beginning. Ever since I got caught up in this business I've been determined — but *determined* — to get at the truth. Somewhere in this world there's a man willing to let you rot for twenty years because of the crime he committed. I *hate* that man. Anyway, the best I could do for a start was to collect all the newspaper accounts of the case. That took weeks.'

'You could have seen the file copies at the newspaper offices.'

She shook her head. 'That didn't suit me. I wanted to study them at leisure. Fortunately, most of the family had kept their copies, but it meant writing round — and that's what took the time. Still, I got a pretty fair collection in the end. Well, now we come to the interesting bit. I'd been reading through them one day, and chucking each one down on the floor when I'd finished with it. They fell all higgledy-piggledy and, when I looked down, that photograph was half-covered — like it was just now. My first thought was that it was a picture of you, and I wondered how I'd come to miss it. Then I moved the top paper and — of course — it was Milo. He really does look like you, if you cover up his chin and his mouth. And that set me thinking. If *I* could mistake Milo for you, so could somebody else. And when I read that the body had been under the eiderdown, I felt sure I was right. What you said just now has proved my point. Are you with me?'

'You're saying that whoever shot Milo thought he was shooting me. But *why*? There must be a motive — and who would want me out of the way?'

She held up a hand. 'I know. I know. You haven't an enemy in the world. But life's not like that, Alan. I should know. Listen, I really am deadly serious about this. If I'm right, you could be in danger at this very moment. And that's why I'm going to tell you what I think. You may not like it, but I'd never forgive myself if I didn't warn you and then . . . ' She left the sentence hanging in the air.

'Go on,' I said.

'Promise not to jump down my throat?'

'I promise.'

She took a deep breath. 'O.K. Here goes. First of all, I thought it must have been Laura. Speak no ill of the dead and all that — but, from what I've heard, she had a pretty possessive nature. If she'd suspected that you were fooling around with Susan Mordant it might have pushed her over the edge. But we can skip my port-mortem cattiness. Laura had an alibi. She was with friends in Westerham all evening. But it was thinking about Laura that put me on the right lines. Remember what I said when you told me your theory about the murder?'

'You said it was too clever. Like something in a book.'

'Yes. But that was when we were thinking of somebody who wanted to kill Milo. There was too much coincidence in your notion that the murderer just happened to have a gun identical to the one in the showcase. But now we're looking the other way. We're after somebody who came to the museum that night in order to kill you. And that makes one hell of a difference. You see, if that business with the gun had been carefully planned, some of the points in your theory still hold good and, what's more, they now make more sense. Using that gun saved the killer getting one of his own — with all the risks that involves — and it saved him the job of disposing of the weapon outside the museum.'

She was going over the old ground I had covered again and again during long hours in my cell. I didn't want vindication for my theory. I wanted to know whom she suspected. If she could believe Laura capable of murder, she could believe anything.

'Never mind why that gun was used. Who used it?'

Her answer came with the impact of a bullet.

'*Hugo Mordant.*'

★　★　★

By the time lunch was over I was able to consider her accusation calmly. It could not have been easy for her to sit there and tell me to my face that one of my friends had attempted to kill me. I credited her with extremely good reasons for making so damning an assertion — and when she had explained her process of deduction I had to admit its validity. As Hugo himself would have said, *Possible, but not probable.*

She had started from the known fact

42

that Laura suspected me of having an affair with Susan Mordant. Indeed, it was more than mere suspicion. My wife had been convinced of my infidelity. On reflection, Dorothy saw that even if Laura had been in a murderous mood, she was more likely to have wreaked vengeance on Susan than on me. That idea started a train of thought which led inexorably to Hugo.

Like anyone else, I have not led a blameless existence, but the only hostility I have evoked from other people has been connected with my work. Archaeologists and historians can be notoriously cantankerous if their pet theses are challenged — and I have slaughtered a few antiquarian sacred cows in my time. But my opponents have never reached for a gun. Their accustomed weapon was a blistering letter to *Antiquity* or an article in one of our professional journals. Dorothy may not have seen me for twenty years, but she did her homework thoroughly, pumping relations for all the family gossip about me. From that she learned that I had lived on an undramatic and humdrum level ever since I came to man's estate. This meant that the only episode in my life capable of arousing unholy passion in anyone was my alleged adultery with Susan. The moment she made that discovery, Dorothy automatically reduced the field to only two runners — Laura and Hugo. Hugo must be favourite, since Laura was disqualified because of her alibi for the night of the murder.

My cousin was watching me anxiously.

'Go on, Alan. It's your turn. Let's have all the objections.'

'Hugo is my friend.'

'Good point. But Laura was your wife — and she believed you'd gone to bed with Susan.'

'Yes, but Hugo didn't believe that. He did his best to make Laura see sense.'

'I'll bet he did. He had to — for the sake of appearances. Listen. Here's how I see it. He'd killed Milo in mistake for you, but by an odd twist you were accused and sentenced. As long as you were alive, there was a chance of things going wrong for him. His safest plan was to keep up the pretence of being your trusting friend. That's what he'd have done if he really had killed you. Any sign that he suspected you and Susan would have made him the obvious suspect.'

That made sense. But there was another objection.

'I spent last weekend with the Mordants. If Hugo hates my guts as you suggest, I'm sure I'd have noticed something. But we were — well, the best of friends. Give me some credit for being a judge of character.'

She seized my hands impulsively. 'Alan, you know your trouble, don't you? You're too trusting. Take Milo Hagerty. There was a man with a criminal record as long as your arm — and what do you do? You invite him to make himself at home in your apartment any time he likes!'

'All right then, why didn't Hugo finish me off over the weekend? If he's as clever as you suggest, he could have arranged an accident.'

She bit her lip thoughtfully. 'I can't answer that one. Maybe he just isn't ready yet. If he's going to try a repeat performance, he'll plan it carefully — down to the last detail. Just like the plot of one of his books. Have you ever read any of his novels?'

'No, I haven't. I don't go much for thrillers — and that's all he writes these days.'

'Well, just you improve your mind. Here, take this.' She fumbled in her bag and handed me a book with a lurid dust-jacket bearing the title *Family Vault*. I glanced at it and let it fall on to the sofa.

'Read it,' she said. 'It'll show you what goes on inside your friend's mind.'

My laugh sounded artificial. 'You're being melodramatic, Dot. If you'd been there over the weekend, you'd see just how cockeyed your suggestion really is. There we were, Hugo and I, nattering away about modern literature. Why, he even wants to use my theory about Milo Hagerty's murder as a plot for one of his — '

'*What!*' She cut in on me, her eyes wide with dismay. 'You mean you *told* him?'

'Why not? You said yourself it was like something out of a book, so I thought — '

'Oh, Alan, you are a *fool*. You really are. Don't you see what you've done? You've shown him that you're half-way to guessing the truth. You only need to look at your theory from a different angle, like I did, and you've got him bang in the middle of the viewfinder. Oh, my God, he really will have to attend to you now. You're too big a risk to leave alive.'

3

Fabius, the Roman general, was wrongly accused of cowardice in his campaign against Hannibal because he consistently avoided direct confrontation. There's a lot of Fabius in me — but in my case there's a fair bit of cowardice, too.

I was not fully convinced by Dorothy's arguments, but sooner or later I would have to come to a decision about Hugo Mordant. I temporised — and I'm particularly good at doing that. Incarceration has taught me patience. For a couple of months I managed to keep my conflicting emotions in balance, telling myself that I was preserving an open mind on the subject. I even engaged in a desultory correspondence with Hugo on the problems I encountered as my book on the centurion began to take shape. When I was alone I reasoned that it would be foolish to jeopardise our friendship on account of an unsubstantiated accusation. But when I was with Dorothy — and that occurred with increasing frequency — I maintained that I was just playing safe and keeping a wary eye open.

She was more concerned for my safety than I. If the hum of the lift heralded a visitor to my apartment she would become tense, and once, when a big Mercedes nearly ran us down as we were crossing Baker Street, she was convinced that Hugo was behind the wheel.

'But that chap had red hair,' I protested as we stood gasping on the pavement.

She looked at me scornfully. 'A wig,' she said.

I still prided myself on my open mind, but on May the thirteenth I knew that I had already come to a decision — almost without realising it.

On that Wednesday morning I received a letter from Hugo asking me to go up to Meden Market for the weekend. Immediately I began to look for an excuse to stay in London. It was true that Dorothy and I had a tentative arrangement to drive down to Rye on Sunday, but I could easily have put that off.

Instinctive reactions are very revealing. I had allowed myself to be persuaded by my cousin's arguments.

So . . . ?

So I should have gone straight to the police and told them of my suspicions. What I had been through gave me justification for doing that. But the shade of Fabius rose before me, and I decided to postpone such drastic action until I had sufficient proof to back up my accusation.

I think *Family Vault* did much to convince me that Hugo's guilt was not only possible, but probable. I found the book unattractive. For one thing, the murderer was the hero. Maybe that's in keeping with modern trends, but I like to identify with my heroes — and this chap was far too unpleasant for my taste. Hugo was clearly delighted with him. You could tell that from his descriptive passages and the way he consistently justified the violence and general nastiness. And the whole story reeked of sex. That surprised me. I had not seen Hugo as one of those writers who protest that sex has been treated as something dirty for too long — and then proceed to make it positively stink in their books. The hero of *Family Vault* was not only a murderer — he was a sadist, and Hugo described his exploits in loving detail. There was an atmosphere of fantasy about that story which I found disquieting. I felt I was looking into Hugo's soul and seeing it as I had seen the Countdown Club on that December morning — shabby, sordid — and slightly disgusting.

I know it's dangerous to confuse an artist with his creation. Respectable clergymen write horror stories, and women of impeccable virtue bring forth fictional lechers — but *Family Vault* was different. In everything the hero said, I could hear Hugo speaking — yet he was saying things which made me shudder. And that's no exaggeration.

I found myself wondering what life with Hugo must be like for Susan — and that was another disturbing experience.

Then I remembered Russell Minty, and immediately I had a strange sense of foreboding. There was a clear parallel between Susan's clandestine encounters with that artist and what had happened with me. If Hugo really had tried to kill me, it could only have been because he had discovered Susan's precious secret — and misinterpreted what he found. That meant Susan was not as discreet as she liked to imagine — and *that* could mean Hugo already knew of her visits to Minty's home. If that were so, the artist could be in danger as great as had threatened me two years before. At last I knew what I had to do. I must go up to Meden Market and warn Minty of the risk he ran by accepting Susan's commission for that portrait. But that would be tricky. The Vicarage was almost within sight of the Mordant house, and it would be difficult to explain to Hugo and Susan why I had visited the village without calling on them. I must avoid arousing suspicion in that quarter. Could I persuade the artist to meet me somewhere else? It was worth trying.

I was on the point of writing him a letter when I hesitated. There was no way of telling what might happen to my letter. Minty might reveal its contents to Hugo. Even if he were wise enough not to do that, it could be just my luck for him to leave the letter lying around in his studio where Susan could see it.

I telephoned.

Meden Market was not on the STD system, so I had to ask the operator for the number and then wait for her to call me back when she had got through.

Minty sounded a pleasant sort of chap.

'You won't know me,' I told him. 'My name's Alan Trevithick . . . '

He interrupted me. 'Ah, but I feel I *do* know you, Mr Trevithick. You're a friend of the Mordants, aren't you? And the victim of a miscarriage of justice, by all accounts. Susan has told me a lot about you. What can I do for you?'

This was not going to be an easy conversation.

'I was wondering if we could meet. There's something I'd like to discuss with you.'

'Any time. I'm in most days. When would you like to come?'

'Well, the fact is, I'd rather not come to your studio. What I mean is, I don't want Hugo and Susan to know I've been in touch with you.'

I could hear him chuckling at the other end of the line.

'If you don't mind my saying so, Mr Trevithick, you're as bad as Susan. What a girl for secrets! Am I right in thinking you have a commission in mind?'

This was awful.

'Well . . . no. It's a personal matter — of some urgency.'

There was a slight pause before he spoke again. 'I see. Couldn't we deal with it now?'

'Not on the phone. It's . . . well, rather a delicate matter. Look, I'm not trying to be mysterious, but it really is important that we meet.'

This time the pause was so long that I began to wonder if we'd been cut off.

'Are you there?' I said, anxiously.

'Yes, I'm still here, Mr Trevithick. May I ask you one question?'

'Go ahead.'

He spoke slowly, as though weighing

his words carefully. 'This delicate matter you mentioned. Would it have anything to do with Susan?'

It was my turn to hesitate. In an intuitive flash I realised the implication in his words. I would have to be careful. As it transpired, I was not careful enough.

'That's a loaded question, Mr Minty. What I'm talking about does concern Susan, yes. But it really concerns Hugo more. Do I make myself clear?'

As soon as I heard him speak I knew that I had bungled things.

'Abundantly clear, Mr Trevithick. I may add that you're not the first. I've already had a bellyful of well-meaning advice from my neighbours, and I'll just content myself with telling you what I told them. Mind your own business. Good night, Mr Trevithick.'

The line went dead.

★　★　★

At a quarter to ten the next night I was ringing Minty's doorbell. The door opened and I had my first sight of the artist. He was shorter than I — about five feet nine I should say — and dressed in shabby tweeds. His appearance was that of the traditional country gentleman. Only the long red hair and beard, which gave his delicate features a Christ-like quality, betrayed his chosen profession.

'Yes?' Obviously he did not know who I was.

'I apologise for this late call, Mr Minty. I'm Alan Trevithick. I think we got our wires crossed last night, but it's vitally important that I see you.'

He stiffened slightly. 'Well, now you've seen me.' He wasn't giving an inch. I had to get through to him quickly before that door closed.

'I haven't driven all the way from London just to join in the chorus of village gossip. I believe you're in very great danger. The same danger that put me behind bars.'

To my surprise and relief, his face relaxed into a smile.

'Mr Trevithick, you intrigue me. You're enigmatic. You're persistent. And I think I've misjudged you. Come on in.' He stood aside to let me enter.

'Now,' he said when we were settled in front of a glowing log fire in his miniature drawing-room. 'Unburden your soul.' He leaned back in a large armchair and regarded me with twinkling eyes. I had rehearsed my speech carefully.

'I don't know how much Susan has told you about me, but three years ago she started writing a book about the Spanish Armada. It was supposed to be a great secret. She wanted to surprise her husband by getting it published without his knowledge. I think she dreamed of presenting him with an autographed copy on the morning of publication. She needed advice on a number of technical points, so she came to me. I was a museum curator — and I do know quite a bit about Spain. We met often, and she sometimes stayed in my rooms at the museum until quite late at night when we were working together on some special line of research. One night at half past nine she came to my apartment while I was out of town. She found the body of a fellow called Milo

Hagerty. You know all this?'

He nodded.

'Well, that was the end of our innocent little conspiracy. She packed in her writing and told Hugo exactly what had happened. It was also the end of a number of other things. My freedom and my marriage in particular.'

'She told me that, too.'

'But there's one thing she hasn't told you, Mr Minty. It was very nearly the end of my life.'

He raised a quizzical eyebrow. 'Is this dramatic licence, Mr Trevithick?'

'Not a bit. If I hadn't missed my train in Leeds, I'd have been in that apartment, and I would have died instead of Milo Hagerty. He was killed in mistake for me.'

'Remarkable. I had not realised that museum curators live so dangerously. Whom had you offended?'

His placid tone riled me.

'Hugo Mordant,' I said.

He frowned and stroked his beard. 'A bit out of character for Hugo, wouldn't you say?'

'I might have done — before I

reconsidered the evidence . . . and before I read his latest book.'

'*Family Vault*? Huh! Sensationalism. You surely don't regard that singularly unpleasant book as Hugo's self-portrait?'

'Something like that.'

'Then you clearly have much to learn about human nature. Merciful heavens, I should hate to think that criticism of my art is judgement on my character. My *Grecian Urn* was branded as obscene by one fool of a critic. Does that make me the sort of man who scribbles on lavatory walls?'

'This was different. Mind you, I didn't just read the book for entertainment — as you would have done. I wanted to see what it would tell me about Hugo.'

'And no doubt you found what you expected to find. It's a common enough mistake in the field of psychology. Freud was one of the worst offenders. Once he'd propounded his theory he interpreted every new piece of evidence in such a way that it *had* to fit in with his scheme of things.'

I shook my head. 'I don't know about

that. In any case — I hadn't made up my mind about Hugo before I read his book. And I certainly didn't find what I expected. Far from it.'

He placed his fingertips together and rested his head on his hands, almost as though he were praying. Perhaps he was. After a few moments he looked up again and regarded me steadily.

'Why tell me all this?' he asked. 'If what you say is true, how d'you expect me to help you?'

'I don't want your help. I came here to warn you.'

He frowned. 'I'm sorry if I appear obtuse, but I don't see the connection. Are you saying that Hugo is likely to go berserk and clobber me with a golf club?'

'It could happen. The point is that I believe he tried to do me in because he thought I was having an affair with his wife.'

'Ah!' The sound came like a long sigh. 'I begin to see daylight. You're saying that because Susan comes here to sit for me, Hugo may suspect an amorous intrigue.' He over-emphasised the last words like a ham actor in a French bedroom farce.

I stood up. 'I'm wasting my time,' I said shortly. 'I'd hoped to convince you of the danger, but you're as blind to the obvious as I was two years ago. I'll be on my way.'

He waved me back to my chair. 'Sit down, Mr Trevithick, sit down. Don't mind me. I have an unfortunate habit of appearing flippant. Susan is always chiding me for it. I'm not blind to the obvious — and, even if I were, I think my eyes would have been opened during the past few weeks. Several of my neighbours have tactfully suggested that my professional association with Susan Mordant could be interpreted as indiscretion. Even my good friend the Vicar has given me a few words of fatherly advice.'

'He would,' I said with heavy sarcasm, remembering what I had suffered from the well-meaning chaplain.

'Ah, don't misunderstand me. He was not pontificating on my moral condition. Far from it. He's an understanding fellow. Been most things in his time — before he turned his collar back to front. Soldier . . . actor . . . yachtsman. Quite a lad. No, he just dropped the hint that tongues were wagging in the village. He's doing his best to make the local peasantry realise that the twentieth century is actually with us. Most of 'em aren't even convinced that Queen Anne's dead. But all that's by the way. No, I'm not blind to the fact that local gossip has already tucked Susan and me into a snug and sinful bed. But surely Hugo is different. He's a writer, not a frustrated village spinster. We artists must stick together. But I see my oratory does not bring tears of conviction to your eyes. You're bursting to tell me this is exactly how you felt two years ago. Right?'

I nodded.

'Hmm,' he murmured thoughtfully. 'So where do we go from here? I think we've reached a stage in our deliberations where a drink is called for. What'll you have?'

'I'm driving.'

'You're surely not going back to town tonight? I've a spare bed. Doss down here, and welcome.'

'I dare not.'

'Dare not? Strong words, Mr Trevithick. Have no fear. I shall sleep by your door with one eye open and an unsheathed Luger in my hand. Hugo Mordant shall be denied his prey this night.'

I laughed. Russell Minty's sardonic humour was beginning to grow on me.

'I just don't want Hugo or Susan to know I've been to see you. I've already turned down their invitation for this weekend, and if I'm spotted leaving here in the morning the proverbial cat will be out of the bag. Hugo would be bound to suspect that I'm on to him.'

'Pause for refreshment,' he said, gesturing towards the table on which was ranged an inviting array of bottles. 'What's it to be?'

I settled for whisky. When he was back in his armchair he asked, 'D'you mean he doesn't suspect already?'

'I doubt it. He'll think I'm too dim to see he's the only person with motive, opportunity and ability to kill me. He wouldn't be wrong, either. I didn't work it out by myself.'

Minty sipped his drink. 'My own dimness surpasses belief. Enlighten me. How did you come to suspect Hugo? You must have a damned good reason. After all, you're supposed to be his friend.'

I told him.

When I had finished he sat silent, bent forward in his chair with his glass pressed to his forehead as though to cool his brow.

'Almost thou persuadest me,' he murmured, without looking up. 'But what's to be done? I can't abandon Susan's portrait. It's nearly finished. Ah, maybe that's the answer. Once she's given it to Hugo he'll know why she's been coming here, and that will be the end of the matter. Or, better still, I'll ask her to tell him straight away. Where there's no secrecy, there's no cause for suspicion. How about that?' He sat back in his chair.

'There's a snag,' I pointed out. 'What reason would you give Susan for insisting that she tell Hugo at this stage in the proceedings? She'll hardly believe you've developed scruples about secrecy after all these months.'

'True.' He sighed. 'Damn it, Trevithick, you're a disturbing influence. I live a nice ordered existence here. But now . . . ' He ran a hand through his long hair in exasperation. 'Ah well, I'll just have to finish the portrait as quickly as possible.'

'And take care,' I added.

'Your concern touches me — but let us be practical. Just how do you suggest I take care? I must appear to carry on as normal. D'you realise what that means in this backwater? Our sort of people are thin on the ground, y'know. Don't think I'm being snooty, but if I want decent intelligent conversation — and a man *needs* that, Trevithick — I can only get it in three or four houses. The Vicarage next door is one, and Hugo Mordant's is another. He may ring up tomorrow and ask me over for a drink. Do I refuse? Look here, what are *you* doing about all this? It's much more your problem than ever it is mine. Hugo's done nothing to me — but you reckon he tried to kill you . . . and when that failed, he let you go to prison for what could have been the best part of your life. It's all very well you

65

coming to me with your 'Heed the gipsy's warning' patter, but is that all the action you plan to take? What about the police? They're supposed to protect us — but I can't shuffle down to the local nick and cry, 'Save me from the clutches of Mad Mordant!' Old Hugo's a respected citizen in these parts. Sits next to the duchess at tea, and all that. Our local sergeant would wheeze through the fronds of his walrus moustache and mutter, 'Now, now, sir, where's the *hevidence*?' And I haven't a crumb to offer him. But *you* have.'

His brief impersonation had been a little masterpiece of mimicry. For a few seconds, as he puffed out his cheeks and licked an imaginary pencil, he even *looked* like a music-hall copper. But there was truth in what he said.

'That's just the trouble,' I admitted. 'I don't have the sort of evidence that would hold up in court.'

Minty rose to his feet and kicked a stray log back into the hearth.

'Then I strongly advise you to get some,' he said.

'I intend to do just that,' I promised. *How?*

★   ★   ★

Despite his pressing invitation, I returned to London that night. As I drove down the Vicarage drive I glanced in my mirror and saw the tiny reflection of his figure silhouetted against the light as he stood at his front door, an arm raised in farewell. That simple gesture awoke an echo in my memory. I saw the gladiators in the hot sand of the arena, their arms outstretched to hail the garlanded figure lounging in the imperial seat. And I heard again the traditional words that turned an *Ave* into a valediction.

'*We who are about to die salute you!*'

4

That promise to obtain evidence weighed heavily on my mind. There was no point in looking for clues at the museum. In two years the setting for the crime had changed out of all recognition. My successor had ideas of his own, and most of the exhibition features had been remodelled along his lines. The firearms display was gone, and my old apartment was now used as storage space. The new curator had a flat in Bloomsbury, close to a rival establishment, and had no call for a suite of rooms at the museum.

Reluctantly I admitted to myself that if I wanted evidence I could only hope to find it in the lair of my quarry. Elbowing Fabius aside, I put through a call to Meden Market.

'Hugo? Alan Trevithick here. Look, this must sound awful cheek, but may I take you up on that invitation after all? My arrangements have come unstuck at this end, and I really would like to have another session with you about this book of mine.'

My voice sounded false as hell. I'm no actor, but Hugo's response to my deception was as good as an Oscar to me.

'Delighted to have you, Alan. Susan will be pleased. We got your letter this morning and she's been down in the mouth ever since.'

Did I catch a touch of sarcasm in his tone? Anyway, the die was cast, and that same evening — Friday — I drove to Meden Market for the second time in twenty-four hours. Russell Minty could not accuse me of being slow off the mark.

As the Capri swept effortlessly up the M.1 my self-confidence ebbed towards zero. I had deliberately stepped outside my defences to carry the fight into the heart of the enemy camp. That called for a steady nerve and a certain amount of low cunning — qualities to which I make no claim. Worst of all, I had no idea what to look for. From every angle the expedition was ill-judged, but it was the only course open to me.

Saturday was uneventful. In the morning Susan took the Land Rover into Maunsley, the nearest town — some six miles away. I had hoped to go with her, but Hugo offered to vet my manuscript, and as that was my avowed reason for coming up to Meden Market I could hardly refuse him.

Had things been otherwise, that morning would have been a valuable experience. I had never known Hugo more helpful. He took what I had written and breathed life into it. No other description is adequate. Whole paragraphs which had cost me hours of toil were ruthlessly deleted and replaced by succinct sentences which swept the story along with the relentless stride of a Roman legion on the march.

At one point he laid down the sheet he was reading, whipped off his thick-rimmed glasses and massaged his forehead thoughtfully.

'This bit won't do,' he said emphatically. 'The man's a soldier. He simply wouldn't react in that way. Now, wait a minute . . . wait a minute . . . '

His fingers drummed on the desk at which he was sitting.

'Got it!' he exclaimed. 'I have just the thing. It happened in the last war, but you could adapt it. Now let me think . . . what were the details? My memory!' He smacked his brow in mock despair. 'Hold on, though. I wrote it down. Yes . . . of course. It'll be in my plot-book.'

He slid open a drawer and pulled out a battered volume. As the repository for his creative genius it was — to say the least — unusual. I glimpsed the title on the spine. *What Men Know About Women*.

He glanced up and noticed my surprised stare.

'Ah — the title,' he said, with a laugh. 'This book was given me as a joke. You're supposed to leave it lying around for people to pick up. They're intrigued, you see. Expect something spicy. But all the pages are blank. Or *were*,' he added. 'I wasn't going to waste this on randy-minded visitors. These pages are too good to leave unsullied. I've been using this for years.'

'You put all your plots in there?'

'Every one.'

'Did you . . . ' I tried to sound diffident. 'Did you ever get round to that idea I had? You know, about Milo Hagerty's murder.'

Did he hesitate a shade too long?

'Eh? Oh, *that*. Yes, I did jot it down. Just the salient points. But about this other incident . . . ' He flicked through the pages, found what he wanted, and began to rough out an episode for my centurion.

As I sat there, watching him at work, I was seized with sudden curiosity about the contents of that plot-book. What had he made of my theory about the murder? Had he simply noted down what I had told him — or would his version contain some alien element, some echo of what really happened, which would reveal the plot as his rather than mine? It was an outside chance, but where else could I look for the evidence I needed? Before my visit was over, I must see inside the covers of that book.

The afternoon was wet, so we sat in the drawing-room watching some of Hugo's efforts as an amateur film cameraman. His technique had none of the confidence he brought to his writing. The films were little more than a succession of animated snapshots. But for all their faults, they were enjoyable to watch. Apart from shots taken in the garden — Susan watering the flower beds; Susan in a bikini beside the pool; Hugo in shirt-sleeves typing on the terrace — there were some good pictures of their Spanish villa which filled me with nostalgia. They, too, had discovered the delights of Spain and were converting the villa into a permanent residence. Between reels Hugo trotted out all the old clichés about crippling taxation, the cost of living and the shortage of domestic staff — to say nothing of the vagaries of English weather. I reminded him of The Rain in Spain and pointed out that winter was not unknown on the shores of the Mediterranean.

'When d'you plan to move?' I asked.

'Before the autumn,' said Hugo, threading the film through the projector. 'I'm not spending another winter in this planners' paradise.'

The significance of his words only dawned on me halfway through the next reel. My first reaction was relief. With Hugo out of the country, Russell Minty and I would be able to sleep soundly o' nights. Then I saw the sinister implication. If there was any fresh mischief afoot, the blow could be expected at any time. *Before the autumn* — that could mean any time in the next three months.

Hugo was explaining the action on the screen.

'Bought her at the Boat Show last year. Just the job for a layabout like me. Goes through the locks on the canal, motors well on the river — and nips along under sail without lying over on her ear.'

We were watching a shot of Hugo and Susan, dolled up in fancy yachting gear, clambering aboard a Mirror 16 motor-sailer.

'Russell Minty took these pictures,' said Susan. 'You can tell he's an artist. Look how he's composed that shot.'

Hugo grunted. 'Met our local Picasso?'

'Why . . . no.' I saved myself just in time. I had been concentrating on the film, and the question caught me unawares.

'Supposed to be something of a celebrity,' said Hugo. 'Can't say I'd noticed. Pleasant enough chap, though. Comes over once in a while for a drink and a natter. Like to meet him? Could we manage an extra one for lunch tomorrow, Susan?'

My apprehension was mercifully short-lived.

'He's away for the weekend,' said Susan. Was that coincidence — or was Minty taking my warning seriously?

'Ha!' Hugo laughed mirthlessly. 'Trust Susan to know all the village comings and goings. Most of the people round here are strangers to me, but Sue's well up in all the local scandal. Aren't you, my chick?'

To my alert ear there was a subtle inflection even in that term of endearment which robbed it of all warmth. On the screen we could see a washed-out shot of two people struggling to launch the boat from a trailer.

'I got the exposure wrong,' said Susan apologetically.

A succession of white dots danced before our eyes, and a moment later the screen flashed into dazzling whiteness as the end of the film flicked through the gate.

★ ★ ★

At three o'clock in the morning I crept downstairs to the study.

Hugo and Susan made a ritual of watching the midnight movie, and as my first experience of colour TV — it came to the fore during my imprisonment — I had the doubtful privilege of seeing a Western made twenty years before. The hero's six-gun resolved all problems with the serene omnipotence of a classical *deus ex machina*, and we got to bed at half past one.

I had planned to sneak a look at Hugo's plot-book some time next day, but the silence of the house was too great a temptation. I might not have so good an opportunity again.

Downstairs in the hall a clock chimed three as I opened my bedroom door.

The whole operation was almost too easy. Within five minutes I had the book in my hands. All the entries were dated. Hugo had started them in nineteen sixty-three. I turned to the last page, on which he had written some notes on cremation and funeral arrangements. Before that was a collection of anecdotes about cruising. He must have planned a story with a nautical setting after buying his boat. Then, earlier still, came the rough outline of *Family Vault*. That was dated eighteen months before — at the time I was still waiting for my first appeal to come up. So it seemed that Hugo had lied to me about making a note of my murder theory. Why? Politeness? If my suspicions of him were correct, he had no cause for such sentiment where I was concerned. Disappointed, I leafed idly back through the pages — and then I found it. The word *Museum* leaped at me from the page, despite the fact that it had been roughly crossed out. The original title — *Museum-piece* — had been replaced by *Days Among The Dead*. I recognised the quotation. '*My days* among *the dead are passed.'* That summed up my life very neatly.

I skimmed through the entry, holding the book close to the shaded desk lamp as I deciphered Hugo's erratic handwriting. Whatever had possessed him to keep so dangerous a weapon in an unlocked drawer? Was he so confident of his security that he failed to recognise that shabby book for what it was — a Sword of Damocles suspended above his head?

A clever counsel might have made effective use of the argument that the details of Hugo's plot were not identical with the events of that night at the museum. In *Days Among the Dead* the victim was the curator and the murderer an insane archaeologist. The motive was professional jealousy — the weakest part of the plot, in my opinion. But no counsel could ignore the date scribbled beside the title. Those notes had been written six months before Milo Hagerty was killed. They were not a theory about what had happened — they were a blueprint for the murder itself!

My first thought was to leave that house immediately and take the book straight to Inspector Quill. It would have been a dramatic reunion for us! Then I realised the folly of such action. If that vital piece of evidence was to retain its full power, the police must find it themselves in its usual resting place. There must be no risk of Hugo suggesting that it was a forgery and that he had never owned such a volume. Carefully I replaced the book and closed the drawer.

In the shadows, Fabius nodded approvingly.

★   ★   ★

On Sunday afternoon Hugo offered to show me round the church. Susan had no interest in ecclesiastical antiquities and settled down with her *magnum opus* on the merry varlets of Sherwood. Looking back, I think Hugo had counted on her doing that. As we left the house he unhitched a pair of binoculars from the hallstand.

'Marvellous view from the tower,' he said lightly.

I could not have had clearer warning than that — but his words rang no alarm in my mind.

The church had suffered grievously at the hands of Victorian restorers, but there were some interesting effigy-tombs and a gem of a shaft-piscina.

After a long climb in the cool darkness of the newel staircase we emerged into bright sunlight on the narrow platform from which rose the crocketed spire. Hugo had been right about the view. The eye could range across miles of heavily cultivated land out of which man-made mountain ranges heaved upwards. The older pit-tips were already blending with the countryside, and I could well imagine a Council for the Preservation of Industrial England raising a storm of protest at any attempt to level them. Without them the landscape would have been a featureless plain.

Beneath us lay the main road which bisected the village. I could see the Vicarage and the Mordants' house among the trees a couple of hundred yards further away.

'Come round the other side,' urged Hugo. 'You can see across into Derbyshire from there.'

He led the way round the base of the spire. 'Mind your step,' he said over his shoulder. 'The parapet is too low for safety. Keep close to the spire.'

I have a poor head for heights and I agreed with him about that parapet. At some time in the past the level of the tower walk had been raised. But in order to preserve the proportions of the steeple, the crenellated parapet had not been altered. As a result it was only two feet higher than the paving. Were any luckless person to stumble, it would offer no protection. On the contrary, it would merely act as a pivot for a sprawling body, tipping it smartly off the tower and down to the gravestones, ninety feet below.

'Here we are,' said Hugo at last. He leaned against the spire, took his binoculars from their case and scanned the flat countryside. Open fields began at the edge of the churchyard, and on this side there were no houses. Not a soul was to be seen.

He handed me the glasses, looping their strap round my neck.

'There,' he said, helpfully. 'I think you'll find they're set all right. Take a look straight ahead. You'll see the yacht basin down where the canal joins the river. A bit to the right of the old brickyard. Our little craft is the one on the extreme left, away from the pub.'

I could see it clearly. After a few moments Hugo touched my arm.

'Keep looking,' he said gently. 'Bring the glasses down a bit, nearer to the church. See that white gate?'

'Uhuh.'

'Keep coming. There's something you'll find particularly interesting. Our own local Roman villa. You can see its outline quite distinctly in the turf at this time of year.'

Immediately my interest was aroused. I had not heard of this villa. To me, a few humps and ditches in a field — as long as they spell Rome — are as fascinating as the Sistine Chapel to a student of art.

'Where?' I exclaimed excitedly — all thought of danger banished. 'Where?'

'Nearer.' Hugo's voice had an hypnotic quality. 'Keep coming. That's the ticket. Better lean forward a bit. It's quite close to the churchyard. Don't worry. I'll steady you.'

I felt his hand on my shoulder — a gentle, restraining pressure.

When it came, his change of grip was almost imperceptible — a slight shift of position which brought the flat of his hand against my shoulder blade. In that second I knew — *knew* — I was on the brink of death.

The horror of the situation brought inspiration. I was in no position to struggle. Hugo had the advantage. Intent on finding that elusive villa, I had bent forward until I was leaning dangerously over the low wall. Before I regained a safe balance, Hugo could send me toppling to eternity — and no one would ever know what had happened. A tragic accident. The knowledge that Hugo had chosen this side of the tower because there would be no witnesses to my fall gave me just the inspiration I needed. To this day I marvel at the speed with which I reacted. Even as the pressure was increasing on my shoulder I said, 'Hello. There's someone watching us through a telescope.'

Feeling death breathing down my neck, I gave a casual wave to the imaginary watcher. In that instant the pressure on my back slackened. Hugo gave a slight gasp and seized my elbow, pulling me backwards to safety.

'Steady on!' he exclaimed. 'Another few inches and you'd have been over!'

I turned and faced him — too quickly for him to disguise his expression. His tone had been one of genuine concern, but his face gave the lie to his words. His lips were drawn back, and hatred and murder blazed from his eyes. In a second he had recovered his composure. He actually laughed. The sound grated on my jangled nerves.

'My God!' he said. 'You were nearly a martyr to archaeology!'

'I didn't see the villa,' I said plaintively — determined to play out my rôle in the macabre charade.

'Never mind that now,' exclaimed Hugo hurriedly. 'You're white as a sheet, man — and no wonder. Let's get back and have a drink.'

Back on the ground, I nearly asked to see the site of the villa — just to note his reactions — but that would have been pushing my luck. The subject was not raised again that day, and the rest of the weekend passed without further excitement.

I set off for London at eleven next morning.

'Come again soon,' urged Susan as I slid into the car. 'We don't see half enough of our old friends.'

'Yes, Alan. We must have another session with your centurion.' Hugo sounded positively hearty.

In the safety of the Capri I could afford to be daring. 'And I want to see that precious Roman villa of yours,' I said innocently.

Susan frowned. 'Roman villa?' she echoed. Her puzzled expression fully confirmed my suspicions.

'Hugo will tell you about it,' I said, and let in the clutch.

I often wonder what he told her.

*　*　*

Before I had been back in the flat half an hour, Dorothy phoned.

'Thank God you're back safe and sound,' she said. 'I've been worried sick about you ever since Friday. Any news?'

'Plenty. But it'll keep until lunch tomorrow.'

'What's wrong with dinner tonight?'

'Won't your customers complain?'

'What customers?' There was bitterness in her voice.

'Business not so good?' I asked sympathetically. She laughed shortly.

'Let's save my troubles for tonight, eh? I can't even say 'Your place or mine?' I'm a refugee, coz. See you around seven-thirty.'

When she came, she insisted on hearing about the weekend before giving me her own news. My report evoked little sympathy.

'You're a twit, Alan. And don't sit there grinning like an ape. I've no patience with you. You promised you'd be careful — but what do you do? You go shinning up church towers with a murderer and then say, 'Where would you like me to stand so that you can shove me off?' Oh, you . . . you . . . ' She glared at me, speechless.

I tried hard to look abashed for her benefit. After all, she was right. But if you want the truth, I was wallowing in the luxury of having an attractive woman boiling up on my account.

'Anyway,' she continued after a moment, 'the next move is obvious, and I can't see how even you can make a hash of it. You go straight to the police. Now. Tonight.'

I shook my head. 'Not for another fortnight.'

'A *fortnight*? You must be out of your tiny mind. Anything could happen in that time. You said yourself that Hugo might make another move at any moment. Why give him two weeks grace?'

'Because I don't just want the police in

general. I want Inspector Quill in particular. He has all the facts of the case at his fingertips and we talk the same language. But he's off on leave. I phoned the Yard this afternoon. As soon as he gets back I'll ring him again. And don't worry about Hugo. He was dangerous enough on his own ground, but this is *my* part of the jungle and I can't see him trying anything here.'

'He tried it two years ago,' she reminded me.

'Ah, but I was living by a regular routine then. He could plan well in advance. But now I'm all over the place — there's no fixed pattern to my movements. And if I know Hugo, he won't risk anything he isn't able to work out first in every detail. I'm safe enough.'

I convinced her. I almost convinced myself.

'All right,' she said. 'But what about this other chap? The artist. Mintoe.'

'*Minty*. I think I finally got through to him. He'd taken himself off for the weekend. Anyway, that picture should be finished any day now. Then he should be in the clear.'

How little I knew.

Dorothy's news brought more pressing problems. The Countdown Club had wilted and died. In my innocence I had imagined that *night-club* was a synonym for *goldmine*. Maybe it is — for some. Not for the Countdown. A constant gamble, it could stand only a short run of bad luck. Yet there was a phoenix-like quality about that tatty place. Within a week it was to open again under new management. In that room at the top of the uncarpeted stairs an international consortium — three down-at-heel Sicilians and one English con-man — were already pouring a libation of vodka down their throats to the success of their new venture. Below stairs the customers would hardly notice the difference. The decor would be unchanged — and morning after morning the same fat cleaner would go about her thankless tasks under the gloomy eye of the dissipated bruiser.

But in the blaze which brought the

phoenix to birth, Dorothy's job had gone — together with the savings of twenty years.

'What about your show?' I asked. She shrugged.

'They know which side their bread's buttered. They'll stay with the Countdown at less than I was paying 'em — and think themselves lucky. So they are. It's a lousy show. God knows why I've bothered with it so long. It's been dying the death for months — years. Be thankful you never saw it.'

'What now?'

She raised an eyebrow. 'I was hoping you might come up with something. At the moment I'm camping out in a hostel. Everything's happened so quickly.'

'Why didn't you tell me before? Maybe I could have helped.'

'You'd have wasted your money.' She stood up and stretched herself. 'Let's not look back. The past's dead. What shall we do, Alan?'

She had asked that question so many times before and, on those far-off holidays, she had always answered before

I could think of anything to say. Usually some outrageous suggestion, calculated to arouse the ire of authority in the form of our parents. Life with Dorothy was never dull. In my boyish simplicity I dreamed of marrying her, one day. Let psychologists make of that what they will. For me it meant that I would have her as a constant companion. I could think of nothing better. But no man in his right mind would suggest mere companionship to Dorothy now. I found her question disturbing.

'Couldn't you go home for a bit?' I asked. She shook her head.

'I'd love to. Cornwall at this time of the year. Think of it. But here's where it's all happening, so they say. I must see some agents and ring up a few contacts. The trouble is, I've been out of the country for so long. People forget.' She sighed. 'Hey ho. What it is to be an artist. But there's no art in the business these days. All these young scrubbers think about is a five-minute routine twice nightly and cash on the nail at the end of the week. They only use their act as advertisement for . . . well, their other talents.'

'Can I help?'

She regarded me searchingly for some moments before replying.

'How much dare I ask of you? I'm flat broke — and I don't even know if I qualify for the dole — or whatever fancy name they give it these days. Insurance stamps and all that caper are a bit out of my line.'

I was beginning to understand how the Countdown Club had run on the rocks.

Suddenly she said, 'I suppose I couldn't shack up with you?'

'Meaning?'

She laughed. 'Now isn't that typical? Any other man would give a straight yes or no — and put his own interpretation on what I'd said.'

'There *are* complications.'

'Your good name? The family honour?' There was a mocking lilt in her voice.

'Come off it, Dot. That's not what I mean. Of course you can stay here. There's a spare room. But — seriously — is it wise? We're not children . . . '

'You can say *that* again.'

' . . . and whatever *we* may think of the arrangements, other people will have their own ideas. I don't want to mess things up for you.'

She reached out and took my hand gently. 'Alan, you know you really are rather sweet. You belong in one of those adventure stories we used to read. Where all the men are terribly, terribly public school and rush around the Continent in Bentleys doing terribly, terribly dashing deeds — but are always terribly, terribly concerned about a lady's good name. Remember?'

'I re-read them every ten years.'

'You *don't*! Oh, Alan . . . how romantic! And is that why you're so bothered about my terribly, terribly immoral suggestion? Actually, all I'm asking is the use of a spare bed. No invasion of privacy, I assure you. Your virtue will remain unimpaired.'

I smiled and squeezed her hand. 'Fathead! Can't you see what I'm trying to say? You're an extremely attractive girl . . . '

'More! More!'

' . . . and if you move in here I might

get out of hand. These things happen.'

Her eyes twinkled. 'You mean I'd have to fight you off? Now that would be something. The last time we scrapped, I gave you a black eye. I don't want to be a nuisance, Alan. It wasn't fair of me to spring my bright idea on you. You've been living like a monk for the past two years and . . . well . . . let's just forget it.' She bit her lip thoughtfully. 'But what the hell am I to do?'

She could not hide her anxiety. Impulsively I spread out my arms in a theatrical gesture.

'All that is mine is thine — even to half my kingdom. Move in when you like . . . stay as long as you like! Only don't say I didn't warn you!'

'You mean that? Bless you! You really ought to run a refuge for fallen women. Seriously — I promise not to be any trouble. No hogging the bathroom; no tights in the washbasin. And I'll dress demurely, speak only when spoken to — and lock my bedroom door every night. How's that?'

I laughed. 'Too good to be true!'

5

The arrangement worked well, but I could not help feeling uneasy. Dorothy had called me romantic, and that was uncomfortably true in a situation bristling with Freudian potential. I had done no more than offer the hospitality of my flat when she was in a fix, but that outraged my code of propriety — and gave me a pleasant sensation of guilt. I almost hoped that some of my old acquaintances would drop by, see how the land lay, and jump to the wrong conclusion. It would boost my ego no end to be thought a hell of a fellow. But there were subtler temptations. I felt sorry for Dorothy in a dangerously protective way. How easy to confuse these emotions with love. Better men than I had made that mistake.

As children we had been close companions, but how little we now had in common. Personal involvement could prove disastrous. Yet in the early hours of the morning, as I sat doodling when I should have been marching my centurion north to The Wall, I could persuade myself that life together would be wonderful. I pictured her asleep only a few feet from where I sat, and the thought made havoc of my careful reasoning.

At times, life could be very complicated.

On the day Inspector Quill was due back from leave I telephoned New Scotland Yard — and missed him by half an hour. He had gone north — the cautious voice at the other end of the line would not be more specific about his destination — and might be away for a couple of days. I could not risk missing him again, and left a message for him to ring me on his return. He did better. He came a-visiting. It was quite like old times.

Dorothy and I were having late breakfast when he arrived — looking just as he had done two years before. The bald head, deeply lined face, sardonic smile and piercing eyes made him double to Julius Caesar. A brilliant mind matched his appearance. He, too, could have swayed the Senate. To complete the picture there was no lack of conspirators eager to compass his downfall.

He joined us at the table, accepting a cup of coffee. Any judgment on our domestic set-up remained hidden behind that high forehead. I could detect no insincerity in his pleasure at seeing me a free man — and that made things easier.

He wasted little time getting down to business.

'I've expected a call from you ever since last December,' he said with a touch of reproach. 'Ought you not to be protesting about our failure to bring Hagerty's killer to book? Everybody goes in for protests these days. Why not you?'

'I've been working on the problem myself,' I said, trying not to sound smug.

'Have you now?' He turned to Dorothy. 'He must be hard up for a job, Miss Merrack. Have you been encouraging him in his folly?'

'She put me up to it,' I said before my cousin could reply. He smiled.

'There speaks the eternal Adam. '*The*

woman *whom thou gavest to be with me, she gave me of the tree and I did eat.'* Well, have you had fun? How long has it taken you to check out Hagerty's contacts?'

I shook my head slowly. 'Guess again.'

He rested his chin on his hand like Rodin's *Thinker* and screwed his face into a caricature of concentration. Dorothy smothered a laugh.

'I give up,' he said. 'You're obviously bursting to tell me. Only — *please* — not suicide. I couldn't bear that.'

I told him.

A good listener, he interrupted no more than twice during the next twenty minutes — and then only to clarify a point.

When I had finished my tale he sat staring into space as though in a trance.

'Go on,' I prompted. 'I'm waiting for the *coup de grace.* Where's the vital flaw? Don't spare my feelings.'

He stared through me for some moments. Then his pupils slowly shrank into focus.

'It's ridiculous,' he said. 'Theatrical

. . . far-fetched . . . too clever by half. But — ' He took a deep breath. 'I can't find a flaw in it anywhere.'

'So what now?'

'We must have that book. Tell me about it again. What else was in it — apart from the plot for the museum murder?'

'Heavens! I can't remember. Practically everything Hugo has written, I should say. I only wish I'd thought to make a copy while I was on the spot. There was the plot for his latest book, *Family Vault*, and an outline for a boating mystery. Then there were some notes on cremation and — '

'Hold it!' Quill spoke sharply. I stared at him. 'I'm sorry,' he said. 'But there's a remarkable coincidence hovering around. Listen. What I'm going to tell you is strictly confidential, but I feel I owe you something on account of what happened two years ago. In any case, you are assisting us with our enquiries.'

'That has an ominously familiar ring about it,' I said grimly. 'What's this coincidence?'

He did not reply at once, but stood up,

walked over to the window and gazed out at the traffic in the street below. Then, without turning round, he told us.

On the day he returned from leave he had been called north to Grimsby on a case which seemed tailor-made for his department. Initially, the facts were simple. A fishing boat had returned to port with an unwanted catch — the body of an elderly woman. The corpse had not been improved by immersion in the sea for over a week, but there were no signs of violence, and superficial evidence suggested that the woman was the victim of an accident. But the police do not rest content with superficial evidence, and closer examination revealed certain singular facts. Indeed, the case became more bizarre at every step.

In the first place, the woman had not drowned. She was dead before her body entered the water. That in itself was strange, but not sinister. The corpse was naked, but the sea can quickly strip a body. In the case of a woman, the mighty deep shows a certain delicacy where nylon underwear is concerned and will coyly leave a pair of briefs in place for weeks. However, the old woman was unlikely to have favoured such scanty attire, so no significance could be attached to the nudity of her corpse.

Identification was difficult. The face was unrecognisable and the mouth toothless. Dentures come adrift easily, even without the aid of decomposition.

An official pen was poised to write the pathetic epitaph, 'Body of Unknown Woman', when a zealous sergeant noticed the wedding ring. Within ten minutes it lay on his desk, smelling faintly of disinfectant. Its outer surface was worn and anonymous — but on the inside of that gold band, still as bright as on the day it first encircled the finger of a young bride, there had been engraved five letters and a date. J.H.P. — M.H. 3.8.14.

In Grimsby and London the teleprinters hammered, and a young constable was despatched to Somerset House to discover who was united in holy wedlock on that sunny August day which was the eve of the war to end war.

When Quill told me the result of that

search I could understand his interest.

Only one couple had the right initials. John Henry Porter, occupation coal miner, had been joined in holy matrimony with Mary Hemmings, spinster and domestic servant. John Henry was a widower, so it seemed reasonable to suppose that he took his bride back to his house, No. 14, Portland Terrace, Meden Vale, in the parish of Meden Market.

Up to that point the search for the identity of the body had been routine. Then — suddenly — Inspector Quill was speeding north. The police at Meden Market were not at all surprised to learn that Mary Porter was dead. She had died in her old-fashioned colliery house three weeks previously. *And her body had been cremated at Maunsley Crematorium.*

Quill turned to face us. 'What did you say was in that plot-book?'

'Notes on cremation and funeral arrangements,' I breathed. The room had suddenly become unbearably quiet.

'Now isn't *that* a coincidence?' said Quill.

The trouble was . . . it just didn't make sense. That sort of mystery bore the unmistakable stamp of Hugo's literary style — a touch of the weird, the seemingly impossible — but there was no reason behind it. What had Hugo Mordant to do with this old widow in Meden Vale? I had glimpsed madness in his eyes, that Sunday afternoon on the church tower, but what kink leads a man to monkey around with a harmless corpse?

Dorothy said, 'I don't like it. I've read enough stuff by Hugo Mordant to recognise his hand in this cockeyed business. Obviously this old woman wasn't cremated at all. Who says she was?'

Quill flopped into an armchair. 'Just about everybody,' he said. 'The undertakers screwed her down, so there's no doubt she was in her coffin. Then they saw her safely to the parish church for the funeral, and on to the crematorium for what they call the committal.'

'Straight into the oven?' I asked. Quill shook his head.

'Not quite. This may be insignificant, but one of the furnaces had been dismantled for repairs, so the coffins were queuing up.'

'Sounds like a black comedy,' said Dorothy. 'Could she have been removed then — before the coffin was put in the furnace?'

'The chap on duty at the crem is ready to swear that nobody touched the coffin.'

My cousin reached out for the last piece of cold toast. 'The coffin was empty when it arrived at the crematorium.'

'Sorry,' said Quill. 'That's out of the question. The bearers would have noticed as soon as they lifted it from the hearse. And there's another thing. The crem people took a full quota of ashes from the furnace.'

'Ha!' exclaimed Dorothy, through a mouthful of toast. 'Joints of meat. I read a story once. There wasn't a body at all, only pork chops and shoulders of lamb. Hawkeye the Detective recognised the bones when they examined the ashes.'

'You must have read that one a long time ago,' said Quill heavily. 'Nowadays the ashes are shoved through a pulveriser and come out like powdered cement. Anyway, it still wouldn't make sense. Why spend God knows how much on meat — and draw attention to yourself — just for the sake of dumping an old woman's body in the sea? And it really was Mary Porter. She fractured her right femur last year and it didn't knit properly. Our P.M. X-rays check with those in Maunsley Hospital.'

I shifted in my chair and leaned towards the inspector. 'Let's get this straight. There were ashes — so there must have been a body. And it couldn't have been the body of poor old Mary Porter. So who . . . ?'

'*Oh, God!*' Dorothy clapped a hand to her cheek. '*Russell Minty!*'

★   ★   ★

'Hold hard.' Quill was not to be stampeded. 'We have no reason to jump to that conclusion. As far as we know,

105

Minty is alive, well, and living in Meden Market. But I'll check as soon as I get back to the office.' He glanced at his watch. 'And that means now. But first — that plot-book. We ought to have it straight away, but if I send someone along for it, friend Mordant will know that we have our beady eyes on him. Everything's still in the enquiry stage and I'm in no position to apply for any sort of warrant, so he could be off into the blue at a moment's notice.' He bit his lip. 'Damn! I've got a feeling about this business, but that's not enough for our hierarchy.'

Dorothy said brightly, 'Suppose Alan says he thinks the Mordants have heroin on their premises. You could get into the house under the provision of the Drugs Act, couldn't you?'

Inspector Quill drew in his breath with a sharp hiss. 'You mean to be helpful, Miss Merrack, but that won't do, you know. To begin with, it wouldn't be true — and that *does* matter, at least where I'm concerned. Secondly, if I were to agree, I'd be guilty of conspiracy. And thirdly, there's been so much hoohah about that sort of thing in the press and on TV that every hack journalist and chat-man in the business is on the look out for it. Two years ago it was police brutality. Last year it was police corruption. This years it's police victimisation. We're fair game. But verily our lot is not a happy one.'

'*I* could get that plot-book for you,' I said, with more confidence than I felt. He looked at me shrewdly.

'You could, at that. But say no more. There are things a well-brought-up policeman should not hear. Once I'm through that door you can say what you like and do what you like. Let me just say two things. *One:* I should dearly like to see that book. *Two:* I can't be party to any illegal act. Do I make myself clear?'

'Abundantly.' I grinned at him. 'I'm a law-abiding citizen. But if it should just happen that . . . '

'No!' he interrupted, covering his ears with both hands. 'I'm one of the Three Wise Monkeys. I hear no evil. Now, back to my cage.' He picked up his hat and strode to the door. With his hand on the knob he turned and faced me. 'Of course . . . if you *should* find any evidence, ring me straight away.'

I flicked up a mock salute. 'Sir!'

'Carry on,' he said. The door closed quietly behind him.

* * *

'Let's go over it just once more.'

We were parked in a narrow lane a couple of miles from Meden Market, and I was more nervous than I cared to admit. Dorothy was listening patiently as I rehearsed — for the tenth time — the details of Operation Book-snatch.

After Quill's departure the previous day she had cursed my folly in offering to get the vital evidence — yet in the next breath she was demanding a share in the enterprise. Now we were about to put our scheme — and our acting ability — to the test.

'Remember,' I said, 'the first stage is to get Hugo into his study. That's largely up to you. Our line is that you're my secretary and that we're on our way to

York. I've just told you that the famous Hugo Mordant lives over in Meden Market, only a few miles off our route. You're dead nuts on his books, so you've persuaded me to introduce you. It's all been arranged on the spur of the moment, and we have to be in York by half past four. Right?'

'Check. So I twitter about longing to see the holy of holies where the great man works. Don't worry . . . I'll get him into that study.'

'And I come, too. But I'm not particularly interested. Hugo knows I don't go much on the stuff he writes. So I prop myself up by the bookcase. He has some stuff on Roman antiquities and I can get engrossed in my pet subject. That's when you ask to see the garden . . . '

' . . . which I feel I already know so well from reading *Family Vault* . . . blah . . . blah . . . blah. Leave it to me.'

'Will do. Gallant Hugo will take you outside, and I shall nip across to his desk and grab the book.'

'Concealing it in the poacher's pocket

of that disgusting old jacket you're wearing. Now, are you sure about Susan?'

'As near as dammit. She can't stand Hugo's literary lion act. She'll suggest coffee — and take her time getting it ready.'

'I hope you're right. Anyway — my job is to keep Hugo in the garden for five minutes. Right. That's about it. Let's go.'

'I feel sick,' I said — half to myself.

'Out of the car!'

'I'm not going to *be* sick. It's just that I feel — '

'I know how you feel. Out of the car!'

Anything for a quiet life. She came and stood beside me.

'Now,' she said briskly. 'Take a deep breath. That's right. Now let it out. Right out. Come on, come on. Good. Now again. Deep. Keep it up. You've got first-night butterflies, my lad. Relax. It's only a game — like when we were kids.'

'You thought up all the crazy ideas, even then.' The details of this visit to Hugo had been suggested by Dorothy.

'And you always backed me up. Was

there ever a time when we didn't get away with it?'

'No.'

'And that's the way it's going to be today. Come on. Keep breathing. Now, on the command 'Move' we get into the car and set off. And we don't say another word about what we're going to do. We start doing it right away. The play's begun. I'm your secretary — as of now — and we're just making a brief detour so that you can introduce me to the marvellous Hugo Mordant. Right. *Move!*'

In five minutes we were outside Hugo's front door.

'Alan! But how . . . ? Why . . . ?' Susan was flustered by our arrival.

'Surprise, surprise!' I chirruped. 'Just a flying visit. We're on our way to York, and Dorothy here has been badgering me for a chance to meet Hugo. She's one of his fans.'

'Dorothy?' Susan's startled gaze left my face and shifted to the car.

'Dorothy Merrack, my secretary.'

'Dorothy Merrack?' Susan blinked at

me. 'Alan, you're pulling my leg. She's your *cousin*!'

Blast! How did she know? The newspapers?

Dorothy was getting out of the car. 'You're quite right, Mrs Mordant. I'm the poor relation — but I do happen to be Alan's secretary, too. He's got into the habit of introducing me that way. It saves misunderstanding when we're on business.'

We all laughed.

Then the laughter faded into awkward silence and we stood looking at each other.

Something was wrong.

I cleared my throat. 'May we come in?'

Immediately, Susan became animated again. 'Yes . . . Yes. Of course. What am I thinking of? Only . . . the trouble is . . . well . . . Hugo's not around just at present. He's down in London with his publisher. Some sort of conference on the next book.'

Double blast! This was going to be tricky. I glanced at Dorothy and raised a questioning eyebrow. Her eyes seemed to say, 'Let's play it by ear.'

We followed Susan into the drawing-room. No doubt about it . . . something was decidedly wrong. She was like a cat on hot bricks. For the first time in all the years I'd known her she was embarrassed by my presence in her house. If courtesy had not demanded otherwise, she would never have let me across that threshold — and now she was desperately putting on an act as the gracious hostess. That was the trouble. She was *too* gracious — as though I were a stranger.

'So, you're on your way to York,' she said brightly. 'Business?'

'You know me. *My days among the dead are passed.*' Was it fear that sprang to her eyes at that quotation? The words had slipped out before I remembered that Hugo had used them for the title of the murder story which was never published. Suddenly a jumbled collection of new thoughts rushed into my mind. Could Susan have read that plot-book? Why not? What more natural than that she should come across it one day while Hugo was out? And if she had read it, she must have recognised the similarity between the plot of *Days Among The Dead* and the real-life tragedy at the museum.

'We have to be there at half past four,' I added, remembering our carefully fabricated fiction. That was Susan's cue to suggest refreshment. She ignored it. Instead, she looked anxiously at the clock.

'Oh dear,' she said, with more than a hint of relief in her voice. 'Then I mustn't keep you. Hugo won't be back until after seven. He's gone by train.'

Once more that awkward silence descended on us. I turned to Dorothy.

'Looks as though your luck's out today, Dot. Perhaps we could call in again on our way back.'

'When would that be?' asked Susan, quickly.

'Tomorrow.' It was the best answer I could think of 'What's the best time to catch Hugo at home?'

She thought for a moment. 'Tomorrow? He'll be in all day, as far as I know.'

'Shall we say around three?'

'That'll do fine.' Her face cleared. 'I'll tell him.' She glanced at the clock again.

Dorothy said, 'Could I use your loo before we go, Mrs Mordant?' Behind Susan's back she winked at me. I took the hint.

While Susan ushered my cousin to the cloakroom, I slipped across the hall and into Hugo's study. By the time Susan returned I was back in the drawing-room, gazing intently at an original Matisse.

And fuming with disappointment.

★   ★   ★

We stopped for a post-mortem a mile down the road.

'What a fiasco!' exploded Dorothy. 'I don't know who hammed it most — us or her. What in God's name was the matter with the woman?'

I drummed my fingers on the leather-covered steering-wheel.

'She's read that plot-book,' I said. 'And she's guessed that Hugo hates my guts.'

'What makes you sure of that?'

'I'm not sure. It was just the way she reacted when I said, 'My days among the dead are passed'. That's the title Hugo gave to the museum murder in his plot-book version.'

She lit a cigarette, leaned back against the head-rest and breathed out the smoke in a long sigh.

'I suppose that's about as feasible as anything else in this crazy business,' she said. 'D'you believe that bit about Hugo being in London? It could just have been a clever move to make sure we didn't stay.'

'Maybe. She's afraid of something. That's what makes me think she must have read the book.'

'You've got that book on the brain. Where d'you think it is, right now?'

'Apart from its not being in Hugo's desk, I haven't a clue. The most likely bet is that he's taken it with him. That's logical, if he's having a conference with his publisher about a new book. Maybe he wants to outline the plot — to see if it's worth while going on. He'd need the plot-book for that, I suppose.'

Dorothy wriggled down more comfortably in her seat and closed her eyes.

'I don't see why,' she said. 'Surely, he'd

have all the details in his head.'

I felt increasingly irritable. 'For heavens sake stop pulling holes in everything I say. I'm not a complete and utter idiot, you know. What a mess this has turned out to be. We should be on our way back to London now. Instead, we're landed with another visit to Meden Market tomorrow afternoon. So much for the Great Detective act.'

She reached out and patted my knee.

'Easy, Alan, easy. At least we're not out of the game. What did she say about Russell Minty? Is he alive and kicking?'

'She hasn't seen him for a fortnight. But that could mean anything.'

Dorothy sat upright and turned towards me. 'Tell you what,' she said excitedly. 'We could come back early tomorrow and scout around. See what we can find out about Minty. And I want to know a bit more about that funeral business. If another body was cremated, how was the switch managed? According to Inspector Quill, the coffin was under constant watch from the moment it left the house.'

I yawned. 'Then the answer's obvious. When the undertakers screwed down the lid, the other body — if there was another body — must already have been inside. There can't be any other explanation. Anyway, I've been thinking . . . Maybe we've jumped to the wrong conclusion about all that funeral stuff. It may have nothing to do with Hugo.'

'It was in his book. You saw it.'

I shook my head. 'No. All I said was that he'd made notes about cremation and funeral arrangements. It was Quill who reckoned there was a connection between the two cases. I wish I could remember what those notes were. I didn't take much interest in them at the time.'

Dorothy stubbed out her cigarette and clasped her hands round her knees.

'What if we find out how the trick was done? With the coffin, I mean. If it ties up with what's in Hugo's plot-book, we'll *know* he was in on it.'

I stared at her. '*Find out?* Just like that?'

'Why not? Good heavens, Alan, you've a tongue in your head. Ask. Ask the undertakers. Ask the Vicar. Ask at the crematorium.' She made it sound so easy.

'They'll tell me to mind my own business.'

'Then *make* it your business. Tell 'em you're the old girl's long-lost son — or something. Say you've heard there's been some hanky-panky. Go all up-stage on 'em. Storm about a bit. That'll get 'em talking. You'll see.'

I groaned. 'More play-acting?'

* * *

We drove to York. There was no point in doing anything else, and Dorothy had never seen the city. As we came into the outskirts she snapped her fingers in annoyance.

'Luggage!'

'I knew what she meant. We had none. Our original plan made no provision for an overnight stop, and to be welcome at any decent hotel we would at least need suitcases.

'Not to worry,' I said. 'Remember

Robert Louis Stevenson. '*An inconvenience is only an adventure wrongly considered.*' We'll buy a couple of cases. What will you need in the way of clothes?'

'Nothing. I've no cash to spare — and I'm not putting you to any expense. You can buy me some toothpaste and a brush. That's all.'

'Don't be ridiculous. You'll need a nightdress and a change of clothes.'

'Why? I can sleep in my birthday suit — and I've some paper pants in my handbag. What more does a girl need?'

'You're joking!'

She wasn't.

We parked near the shopping centre. Before we left the car I took her hand gently.

'Let me buy you some things, Dot. Please. Say it's for old times' sake — or a token of gratitude. After all, I owe my freedom to you.'

She looked at me with shining eyes while a smile twitched at the corners of her mouth. In that moment we seemed closer together than ever before.

'All right, Alan,' she said, softly. 'Buy

me some nice things.'

What a golden afternoon that became. There was something childlike in the way she tried dress after dress, coming for my verdict each time. She would have been content with one diminutive pinafore dress and blouse — which made her look about seventeen — but I insisted that she get something special for the evening. I had made up my mind about our evening in York. It was going to be as near perfect for her as ingenuity could devise and money provide. The best room in the best hotel, with the best dinner they could produce. Then — if she felt like it — a show. And if the night was warm and the moon obligingly full . . . a walk beside the river. The perfect evening for little Cinderella Merrack, while the noble and altruistic Sir Alan flaunted his shining armour in the moonlight — asking no reward but his lady's happiness.

Quite a touching prospect.

Her strapless evening outfit took my breath away. For two weeks we had shared the same apartment, strictly observing the unwritten code which served to keep the temperature down to a safe level. It would have been so easy to send it soaring. A touch . . . a gesture . . . a veiled suggestion — and the whole volcano could have erupted. We were not being prudish. We were not even particularly moral. It was a question of integrity. One wild night — instinct told us it *would* be wild — and the world would tumble round our ears. We had rediscovered the special relationship we once enjoyed. The old root was sprouting new shoots, but we knew how tender was the plant we nurtured. Force its growth and it would die. Between us things had always been special — and that was how they must be if we were to look each other in the eyes without remorse.

All this I knew — yet caution scattered to the winds at the sight of Dorothy in that dress. Maybe she did not mean to be provocative . . . but the damage had been done. Deep inside my brain an imp was gibbering, 'You're not in the apartment now. The rules don't apply.'

Dorothy was speaking.

'I asked if you liked it. Come out of

your trance, Alan. You're undressing me with that look.'

★　★　★

The best hotel in York is not the most fashionable. I could make a long list of the amenities which, thank God, it does not provide. There is no discotheque in the basement; no piped music in the bedrooms; no jaded orchestra rendering threadbare snatches from *The Sound of Music* to drown the clatter in the dining-room. And the waiters speak with the homely accents of the broad acres and not the servile continental disdain affected by their more sophisticated brethren.

Long years ago the place had been the town house of an ecclesiastical dignitary — in the days when Church and State were two sides of the same coin and a prince of the Cloth held court to ambassadors and prelates alike. No latter-day vandal has laid improving hands on the gracious suites. The rooms we occupied retain the proportions they knew when used by long-dead emissaries from Rome or Hampton Court.

We talked little during the evening. By mutual consent, all reference to our enterprise was banished from conversation. My cousin's choice of entertainment was unexpected. At her insistence, we threaded our way through the maze of sun-sleepy streets to a shadowy medieval hall where she sat beside me, enraptured by a brilliant performance of all six Brandenburg Concertos. Music is one of my deepest delights, and her obvious appreciation served to draw us closer together. But Bach hands out no aphrodisiac. Only later, when we sat together by the open window of Dorothy's room, did my self-control begin to ebb again.

A gentle breeze wafted the chimes of the city churches to us. Midnight. The only light in the room came from a standard lamp beside my cousin's chair. With a sudden movement she reached out and pressed a wall-switch. Immediately the background vanished in shadow, while the little area around us was spotlit by the high moon. The gentle light drained all colour from the scene, and we sat like figures in an old Victorian photograph. It was the moment for me to make the first move — to cross that bright patch of moonlight and kneel beside her, ready to take her in my arms. But before I could rise, she spoke. She did not look at me. It was as though she were speaking to herself or to the etched towers and spires that rose above the silver rooftops.

'If only this could last,' she said, simply. 'I haven't felt so good for years — and I mean *good*. Alan, I haven't told you how things have been for me since way back when we were kids. And you haven't asked, bless you. I've had to make a living by trying to please other people. There's one golden rule in show business. Give 'em what they want. But nobody gives anything in return. Oh, I've had plenty in my time. Money . . . clothes . . . even had my own car once. But they weren't gifts. They were payment — for services rendered. D'you know, it's years since I had a real present . . . with no strings attached. Then — today, you gave me just that. It's been wonderful. These clothes . . . the music . . . this lovely old place . . . everything. I wouldn't have dared suggest that concert to anyone but you — but I knew you'd understand. And here we are now . . . quite content to sit and talk, and you haven't even hinted at wanting anything in return. God, what a relief!'

I sat there watching her silently. She lay at ease in a great wing armchair, her face in shadow while a shaft of moonlight washed over her white shoulders and the gently-moving contours of her breasts beneath the dark veiling of that revealing dress. Within me an elemental battle was raging.

She turned her head to look at me, and the pale light caught her delicate features.

'Alan?' It was as though she found my silence disturbing. 'I'm right, aren't I? There isn't any catch?'

'Just what sort of catch had you in mind?' I asked. I had meant to appear flippant, but my voice sounded thick, and even I could hear the harshness in my tone.

'Oh *no!*' She seemed to draw back into her chair, and again her face was hidden in the shadow. 'Don't tell me I've been wrong about you. Not *you*, Alan.'

This time I did move, kneeling beside her and gripping those white shoulders.

'What's so different about me? I'm human. D'you think I'm nothing but a dried-up Egyptian mummy? No guts . . . no emotions? For two weeks you've lived in my flat — and every night I've wanted you. And today you buy a dress guaranteed to send me half out of my mind . . . and you lie back in this chair, urging me on with every breath you take — and then you think you've been wrong about me! Haven't you *any* idea how it is for me after two years living like . . . like a monk? That's how *you* described it. You *must* know.'

Beneath my hands her body shook in a shuddering sigh. 'All right,' she said. 'I've got the message. No need to maul me.'

I let her go, and she stood up.

'Let's see,' she said. 'New dress; complete evening outfit, nightdress; negligee; robe case. Oh, and we mustn't forget

127

the meal and the concert. Big spender, Alan. You'll want your money's worth.' I heard the sob in her voice.

Never before had I felt so disgusted with myself. In an instant I was on my feet with my arms around her.

'Dot, I'm sorry. Forget what I said. This isn't the way things go for us.'

She made no movement. For a full minute we stood gazing at each other in the moonlight with an intensity that hurt. What was she thinking?

For me, one thing was certain. I loved her. Quixotic protection . . . companionship . . . lust. I had cannoned off all three deceptive hazards. But what of the delicate balance of our relationship?

As I watched, her face relaxed and she smiled.

'Hello,' she said, as though seeing me for the first time. Her arms went round my neck and I could feel the pressure of her hand on the back of my head, forcing me closer to her. I held her tightly, feeling the hunger, the passion — but, above all, the tenderness of her response. In those moments I knew how empty my life had become. We clung to each other as though all our security depended on the strength of that embrace.

'I'm so sorry,' I breathed. 'I must have been out of my mind. I — '

'Hush!' She stroked my face gently. 'It's all right, Alan. It's all right. Oh, God . . . this is *good*.'

I felt her arms tighten round me — as though she wanted to hurt herself . . . to crush herself against me.

'I love you, Dot.'

She stood back from me, gripping my arms while she stared into my eyes.

'You've taken your time,' she said. 'I knew I loved you twenty years ago.' Without any warning she laid her head against my shoulder and began to sob bitterly. 'Don't ever let me go,' she cried, her voice muffled in the folds of my jacket. 'Promise!'

I promised.

6

It needed all Dorothy's power of persuasion to keep me from abandoning our quest. At breakfast I was all for driving straight to London and making the necessary arrangements for our wedding. Her argument against that was twofold.

'Of course I want to marry you as soon as we can fix things, Alan, but let's not start off in some tin-pot Registrar's. It doesn't have to be a white wedding, but I want to be married at home in Listhowal Church — and that means a trip to Cornwall and a licence. Point One. Point Two: We can't just drop out of what we're supposed to be doing. That would be selfish — and dangerous. You're not safe while Hugo Mordant is still on the rampage, and the only way to clobber him is to collar his plot-book as soon as possible. And I'm worried about Russell Minty. We agreed to snoop around today to see if he's still in the land of the living.'

So we took the Golden Road to Meden Market. I was elated. How could the world change so radically in so short a space of time? Was this bright highway the same soulless road we had travelled the previous afternoon? To express my new-found delight, I burst forth into an abandoned rendering of Gilbert and Sullivan.

'Brightly dawns our wedding day . . . '

Dorothy bore the affliction bravely. After a while she said, 'You'd better start getting into character.'

'Huh?'

'We're going a-hunting. Remember? And if you're going to get complete strangers to reveal their dark secrets about old Mary Porter's funeral, you must convince them of your *bona whatsits*. You'd better be a nephew. Yes, that's it — a dear, devoted nephew, full of sound and fury because of all the unpleasantness that's come to light over in Grimsby.'

'We're not supposed to know about that. Quill said the information was confidential.'

She eased off her new shoes and wriggled her toes. 'I don't see that it matters. After all, if the police have already questioned the people we're going to see, the cat must be out of the bag.'

'Not necessarily. The police don't always tell you *why* they're asking questions.'

'Then we won't either. We can say we're making our own enquiries, but the police have asked us not to discuss the matter. And that's true. It'll sound good, too.'

She was right. We tried it out on the undertaker and it worked splendidly. He oozed professional unction, expressing his condolences and deeply regretting that we had not been informed of the funeral arrangements. The Deceased Lady (he spoke the words in reverent tones — you could almost see the capital letters) had lived alone, and none of her neighbours knew anything of her family. Some years before she had made provisional arrangements with his firm, expressing her preference for cremation and giving details of the insurance which would pay the funeral expenses.

He angled for information.

'When the police were here, sir, they declined to inform me of the nature of the — er — irregularity into which they were enquiring. I sincerely trust that my professional services are not in question. All our arrangements were carried out with — if I may say so — our customary decorum and reverence.'

I smiled reassuringly. 'As far as I know, this matter does not involve anything like that. But perhaps you could just tell me what arrangements were made for my aunt's funeral.'

'Indeed . . . most certainly . . . yes. One moment while I consult my records and I can give you the complete details.'

He produced a large volume bound in purple cloth. 'Here we are,' he said, licking a podgy finger as he turned the pages. 'We were informed that the Deceased Lady had passed away by one of the neighbours. I went to the house myself, with our Mrs Barton, who obliges us at such times, and took the necessary measurements. That was on . . . let me

133

see . . . Friday the fifteenth. Nearly three weeks ago. We took the coffin to the house on the Monday afternoon, and the funeral was on the Wednesday — the twentieth.'

That seemed straightforward. 'You fetched the body on the Wednesday, then. And went straight to the church?'

The undertaker shook his head. 'No, sir. You must understand that it was somewhat inconvenient for us with there being no family at the house — and I'm bound to say the Deceased Lady's neighbours were not as considerate as they might have been. Somehow it did not seem a good idea to leave the coffin unattended in the house from Monday till Wednesday, so we brought the Deceased Lady here. We have recently opened a most tasteful Chapel of Repose.'

This was a new complication. I wondered if the police were aware of it — and if they appreciated its possibilities.

'Yes,' continued the undertaker. 'We could not take the body into the church, as used to be the custom before we had the Chapel of Repose. You see, it so happened that Sir Henry Bonzell's funeral was on the same day, only earlier. So you might say it was providential, our having the Chapel of Repose available.'

I tried to picture what had happened.

'You mean the coffin was here, on your premises, from — when? Monday afternoon through to Wednesday morning? What are your . . . ' — I was trying to think of the mortician's equivalent of 'security measures' — ' . . . your usual arrangements in such cases? When do you close for the night?'

He frowned. 'Do you mean our establishment, or the Chapel?'

'Both.'

'We usually close the establishment around six o'clock. But you must understand that we are not clock-watchers. If duty demands, these premises are open. Sometimes we do not close until eight o'clock. As for the Chapel, that is almost a separate entity. The bereaved are, I feel, entitled to reasonable access to it at any time.'

'D'you mean it's unlocked at night?' I asked, trying not to sound too eager.

'Not exactly. But the key is available. The key to the side door. I should explain. That door leads directly into the Chapel from the yard at the side of the building. We always use that door for loading and unloading. The doors between the Chapel and the other premises are, of course, locked whenever we close for the night.' He smiled thinly. 'We keep money and items of some value in the office safe here, so we cannot afford to take chances. But there is — and I say this with a due respect for The Departed — nothing of real value in the Chapel.'

Somebody thought otherwise, I reflected.

'While Mrs Porter — my aunt — was here . . . those two nights . . . when were the Chapel doors locked?'

The undertaker looked uncomfortable. 'That I really could not say, sir. It so happened that on both those nights I locked up the office at about six, but two of my assistants worked late in the shop at the back. We were rather busy at the time. They went out through the Chapel and locked up behind them. I should add that their last duty is to switch on the burglar alarm. Were any door or window to be forced during the night, the whole neighbourhood would know. Believe me, our alarm bell is guaranteed — if you'll forgive my little joke — to wake the dead! Yuk! Yuk! Yuk!'

I had to look closely to convince myself that he was, in fact, laughing. The spasm passed, and his face regained its usual appearance of *rigor mortis*.

'Forgive my asking, sir,' he said. 'But is this important? Has anyone complained that they were unable to pay their respects?'

He was beginning to sound affronted. I would have to be careful.

'It's quite all right,' I said blandly. 'I'm just interested in all the details . . .'

Dorothy spoke up quickly before I floundered. 'It's so comforting to know that everything was arranged so beautifully,' she said sweetly.

The undertaker radiated funerary joy. 'It is most gratifying to hear you say so, madam. Would you . . . would you care to see our Chapel of Repose?' He spoke as though we were being accorded an enormous privilege. I nodded, and he led the way through a door at the back of his office.

The Chapel of Repose was a small room panelled in light oak and looking like a stand at an ecclesiastical furnishers' exhibition. At one end a simple table pretended to be an altar, complete with cross, candlesticks and flower vases in lacquered brass.

The flowers were plastic — and entirely in keeping with their setting.

Every door was discreetly veiled by light blue curtains. '*Madonna blue*,' explained the undertaker in a reverent whisper. There were half a dozen chairs, each with a blue — *Madonna* blue — kneeler on which I'll swear no one had knelt since the day it was made.

The middle of the room was occupied — and dominated — by a draped plinth three feet high.

'*The catafalque*,' breathed the undertaker.

'Where the coffin rests?' I asked. He beamed at me and clasped his podgy hands as though in ecstasy. I glanced round the room. 'And people — mourners — come here to . . . what? Pray?'

He smiled at my ignorance. 'Some may, sir. But mostly they come for The Last Look. You know?'

I didn't.

He hastened to explain. 'I fear the custom may be dying out in some parts of the country, but hereabouts the tradition is still as strong as ever, I'm happy to say. It's considered a token of respect to visit the house of sorrow and take a last look at the Deceased Lady or Gentleman as they repose in the open coffin and — ' he leered benevolently ' — I assure you that whatever the cause of decease, my clients invariably present a serene and benign appearance. As I say to every sorrowing relative, 'Rest assured I will treat The Deceased as one of my own family.' ' He flashed his unnaturally white teeth at me.

'Does that not lighten your own sorrow?' he asked.

I glimpsed a vivid tableau of his family — Deceased Ladies and Gentlemen propped round a festive catafalque and supping from lacquered brass vases. The claustral atmosphere of that Chapel was beginning to tell.

I swallowed hard and nodded, wordlessly.

Dorothy said, 'Was Auntie's coffin left open, then?'

He pursed his lips thoughtfully. 'Well, yes and no, as I remember. We were under the impression that there was no family, so it seemed unlikely that anyone would be coming for The Last Look. But, of course, you never can tell. So we left the lid on, but did not fasten it down.'

I was thinking furiously. Here was the weak link in that chain of events which had led from 14, Portland Terrace, to the crematorium. For forty-eight hours that coffin — unfastened — had rested in this room. And one of the doors gave access to the drive at the side of the building. Obviously no one would attempt to tamper with it during the daytime — let alone oust its rightful occupant in favour of another body. The risk of discovery was too great. If the switch had been made here, it must have been at night. What had the undertaker said? Two of his assistants had been in the workshop beyond the Chapel. Hammering? Sawing? Planing? Almost certainly making plenty of noise. If the side entrance was unlocked, anyone could have slipped in and done the job. But it would take time. How long? That depended on the ghoul who was doing it. Manhandling corpses is no light task. *Dead-weight* is a significant expression. Hugo could have done the job, but it would not have been easy. Five minutes? Ten? And whoever did it must have had nerves of pure platinum. Apart from the grim nature of the task itself, that inner door might have opened at any moment.

'Are the lights left on all the time?' I asked, trying to picture the scene as it was during those two nights.

'Oh no, sir. We only switch on the lights when there is need.'

So — it would have been dark. A slight advantage to the intruder if disturbed, but a disadvantage for the job itself.

'I'm a bit concerned about one thing,' I said.

Immediately the undertaker's brow

furrowed with anxiety. 'And what is that, sir? Our one desire is that everything should be entirely to the satisfaction of all concerned.'

'Well,' I said slowly, 'I'm not sure that I like the idea of my aunt's body being in here with that outer door unlocked so that any Tom, Dick or Harry could sneak in.' I glanced at Dorothy for support. She nodded vigorously.

'You read such terrible things in the papers,' she said. What that was supposed to mean I know not, but the undertaker took it seriously enough.

'Indeed yes, sir . . . madam. I take your point. But your fears are groundless, I assure you.' He strode across the room, drew back the curtains and opened the door of the workshop.

'Mr Teazle,' he fluted. A bent figure in a stained apron shuffled forward into view.

'Ar?' it said.

'You were working late when Mrs Porter's coffin was in the Chapel of Repose, were you not?'

'Ar.'

'And nobody came into the Chapel

during that time, did they?'

'Ar.' The minutest inflection gave the sound a negative quality.

'You are quite, quite sure?' The undertaker spoke as to a little child.

'Ar.' Positive this time.

'Because . . . ' here the undertaker leered triumphantly in my direction like a stage magician ' . . . you kept this inner door open all the time, as I have instructed.'

'Ar.' Most emphatic.

'And you switched on the alarm before you left?'

'Ar.' Slightly affronted.

The undertaker closed the door with a dramatic flourish.

'Thank you, Mr Teazle,' he intoned through the light oak panels.

The Madonna blue curtains fell on a muffled '*Ar!*'

'I do hope that has put your mind at rest, sir.' The stage magician was taking his bow. A round of applause would have been sacrilege in that shrine of death. I smiled, but my mind was far from being at rest. My clever theory had been stifled at birth, yet I could not shake off the conviction that the key to the mystery lay close at hand. How had it been done?

Somewhere, another stage magician knew all the undertaker's tricks — and a few more.

*   *   *

It was a relief to breathe fresh air once more, yet, despite my protests, Dorothy insisted that we drive to the crematorium. She did not share my feeling that the mystery centred on the undertaker's establishment.

Maunsley Crematorium overlooks the town from the summit of a wooded hill. The site has been carefully chosen with reference to the prevailing wind, and the building itself is a tasteful blend of brick and stone. At close quarters you could mistake it for a modern church. Even the all-important chimney is cunningly disguised as a bell tower. Unlike some other crematoria, the pseudo-ecclesiastical veneer does not extend to the staff. In place of pale youths in shabby cassocks shuffling a solemn minuet in Gothic gloom to the accompaniment of soulful electronic vibrato, Maunsley boasts a group of dedicated men, healthily robust and clad in sober lounge suits. There is an atmosphere of realism about the place which I found positively congenial and — to my great relief — I was absolved from further deception. The cheerful official recognised me.

'Excuse me, sir, but aren't you Alan Trevithick the archaeologist?'

I was not going to quibble over that description. He reached out to shake my hand.

'John Wade. This is indeed a pleasure, sir. I remember your programmes on the telly. I'm president of our local historical society. We wanted to invite you as a speaker last year, but you were otherwise engaged.' He grinned. I warmed to him immediately. Here was the complete antithesis of the lugubrious, cloying servility of the undertaker in Meden Market.

'I'd be delighted to come,' I said — and meant it. 'Drop me a line and we'll fix something up. Here's my address.' I handed him a card.

'This is my lucky day,' he chuckled. 'But what brings you here, sir? Not archaeology, I'll be bound.'

I explained our mission. There was no point in holding anything back, but I emphasised that Mary Porter's sea-change was a confidential matter. I even admitted to the deception we had practised on the undertaker. He roared with laughter.

'I can just picture it,' he chortled. 'Grief! What a stuffed shirt Henderson is! And it's all for show. He's no more than a figure-head in that business. Oh, he took it on from his father — but the real power behind the throne is old Teazle. That place would fall apart if it weren't for old Chippy.'

'You surprise me. He seemed just a cog in the wheel.'

'That's what makes it all so screamingly funny. Henderson is so pompous — handing out orders right, left and centre — and old Chippy Teazle pulls his forelock and grunts 'Ar!' — and then just goes on in his own sweet way. I hear the lads talking, you know. When they come here, Po-face — that's Henderson — plonks himself down in the front pew of the chapel and solemnly leads off with the responses in the service. But the bearers come in here, once they've brought the cars round to the exit. They've no time for Henderson . . . but Chippy — ah! — that's a different matter. Old man Henderson should have left the business to him. *He* wouldn't have wasted money on that fancy Chapel of Repose.'

'Henderson seems very proud of it.'

John Wade shrugged his shoulders. 'It's a white elephant,' he said. 'And it caused a lot of bother in the village. D'you know, he wanted that place consecrated like a proper church. God knows why. A sort of status-symbol, I suppose. But the Vicar wasn't having it, and the Bishop backed him up. In the end poor old Po-face had to get some back-street Nonconformist pastor to go over and bless it, or whatever these chaps do. I suppose he gave you some long spiel about mourners coming in for The Last Look. Huh! They *don't*. If they're not willing to keep the body at home till the funeral, they're not likely to bother about it while it's in that Chapel. In any case, the usual reason for taking a body to the undertakers is because it's . . . you know.' He wrinkled his nose expressively. 'And when things go *that* way, the best place is a corner of the workshop near an open door. Not in some poky little room. And what if there's more than one body to lie in state? Do they take it in turns, or draw lots for who has the catafalque? You should hear old Chippy carry on about it.'

Dorothy laughed. 'Does he really talk? All we heard him say was 'Ar'.'

Wade chuckled. 'That's when he's talking to Henderson. Get him on his own and he's a regular old chatterbox. But this isn't helping you with your problem, is it? What you want to know is, could there have been any funny business here, after the committal. Frankly — I doubt it. If you've a few minutes, I'll take you round and explain how we do things. Then you can judge for yourselves.'

His conducted tour of the crematorium

was fascinating. I had never been behind the scenes in such a place before. Dorothy was apprehensive, but there was no cause for that. Apart from the chapel, it might have been a factory.

Wade explained the drill. The coffin would be placed on a catafalque (I was becoming familiar with these funereal terms) in a deep apse, like the chancel of a church. At the words of committal . . . 'We therefore commit his body . . . ' the officiating clergyman would press a button on the reading desk and two large curtains would slowly close across the apse, hiding the coffin from the mourners in the chapel. After the service it would be lowered automatically to the furnace-room directly beneath the apse, where an electric trolley would trundle it to the waiting furnace and raise it to the level of the door.

As we stood beside the silent furnace I asked about the unusual delay on the day of Mary Porter's funeral.

'I wouldn't call it unusual,' said Wade. 'We inspect the furnaces regularly, and if there's any maintenance to be done there may be a slight delay. It so happened that on that day we had the Gas Board in, converting the equipment for North Sea gas. They did the other furnace the next day. That's what I mean about there being no chance for any funny business. Two of us were on duty, and there were three gasfitters down here as well, all the time. So nobody could have sneaked in and tampered with any of the coffins, if that's what you're thinking.'

I glanced round the furnace-room and realised the truth of his words. There was no place for an intruder to hide. Mary Porter's coffin would have been under observation the whole time.

'So there was nothing unusual about that particular cremation,' I said, flatly. He gave me an odd look.

'Depends what you mean. I looked through the inspection window a few minutes after the coffin had been put in, and — well — there *was* something a bit odd.'

'Let's have it.'

'Well, I haven't mentioned this to anyone else — not even to the police when they were here at the beginning of the week. You see . . . it sounds a bit daft, but it looked to me as though the body was wearing a duffle-coat.'

I stared at him. 'Are you sure?'

'Well, I can only tell you what it *looked* like. Maybe you don't know what happens when a coffin is put in there. The heat really is terrific. It doesn't take long for the coffin to burn, and then . . .' He paused and glanced anxiously at Dorothy.

'Don't leave me in suspense,' she said encouragingly. He grinned.

'We're used to all this. It doesn't mean a thing to us. Anyway, as I was saying . . . when the coffin gets going, *the corpse sits up.* Something to do with the effect of the heat on the muscles, I believe. I'm almost certain it was wearing a duffle-coat. Certainly not a shroud.'

'Did you see the face?' I asked eagerly. He shook his head.

'No. The hood — and that's what made me think it was a duffle-coat — was sort of pulled forward. No, I couldn't see the face.'

'And you haven't mentioned this to anyone else?'

'No. Why? D'you think it's important?'

* * *

Neither Dorothy nor I had much appetite for lunch.

'I'm more confused than ever,' I admitted as we picked at our pork chops.

She paused with her fork half-way to her mouth.

'Duffle-coat,' she said, thoughtfully. 'That's a clue, Hawkeye. Now all we have to do is find a missing person in a duffle-coat. I know that sounds Irish, but at least it's something definite to go on. The game's afoot — and all that jazz.'

'Hold hard. Before we start capering about after missing persons, we have a job to do. We're getting so mixed up with this cremation business that we're forgetting why we came up here in the first place. Let me remind you that our object is to get hold of a certain book. First things first. As soon as we've finished lunch, we pay our respects to Hugo Mordant.'

7

Susan was full of apologies.

'If only I could have got in touch with you in York,' she said as we sat on the terrace. 'Hugo phoned not half an hour after you left yesterday. He'd decided to stay on in town for another couple of days. That's typical of him. He was sorry to have missed you. I told him about Dorothy. That appealed to his vanity, of course.'

She was more relaxed than on our last visit.

'So it's been another wasted journey for you,' she said sympathetically.

'Not entirely. It's always a pleasure to see you, Susan — and I thought of calling on your artist buddy, Russell Minty. D'you think he's free to accept another commission? Or is he still working on your portrait?'

I watched her closely as I spoke. When I mentioned Minty the colour drained from her face.

'I . . . I don't know,' she stammered. 'The fact is, I haven't seen him for ages. Well, not since before you were here for that weekend.'

I tried to look unconcerned. 'Ah, yes. I remember you saying he was away from home. Hugo wanted him to come for lunch. You mean he hasn't returned yet?'

She nodded. 'I thought he was only going away for the weekend. We'd arranged another sitting, but when I turned up he wasn't there.'

I laughed. 'These arty types. No sense of responsibility. No sense of time, either, by the sound of it. You look worried, Susan. Is this bothering you?'

'Alan, I *am* worried. I can't help thinking something's happened to him.'

'What sort of thing? An accident?'

'Oh, I don't know. Just . . . *something*. I mean, going off like that — and not a word from him since. He usually sends us a letter when he's away — with a little sketch of where he's staying. And he knew about that sitting. It's nearly three weeks now. D'you think I ought to mention it to the police? He hasn't any family . . . and what if he's wandering around with loss of memory or something? If nobody starts asking about him, it could be ages before he's identified. That's an awful thought. Or he might be hurt . . . unconscious . . . No one would know who he is.'

Dorothy said gently, 'They'd identify him by the things he was carrying. A diary, maybe, or some papers.'

Susan shook her head miserably. 'Not Russell. You don't know him. When he takes off into the blue he just slings a few clothes into a kitbag with his painting things, and that's all. He doesn't carry any documents. If you saw him trudging along in that filthy old duffle-coat of his, you'd take him for a tramp or a drop-out.'

That filthy old duffle-coat . . . *Steady, Trevithick! Don't jump to conclusions!*

'What does Hugo say about all this?' I asked.

'I haven't told him. Tell you the truth, Alan, he doesn't care much for Russell.'

'Really? He seemed happy enough about having him over for lunch.'

'Ah, that was different.' She sighed.

'That was the Gracious Host act. All right, I know that sounds bitchy, but it's your fault, Alan. When you first came up here you said Hugo might take a dim view of my going down to Russell's place for those sittings. I hadn't thought anything of it. But then . . . well . . . I began to notice things. The way he speaks whenever he mentions Russell. A sort of sneer, as though he despises him. And he keeps making rotten jokes about 'our local Picasso'. You must have noticed that yourself when you were here.'

'Can't say I remember,' I lied. We were interrupted by the distant sound of a telephone bell. Susan hurried into the house.

'Duffle-coat!' exclaimed Dorothy excitedly. 'I knew it!'

'Take it easy, Dot. Thousands of people wear 'em.'

'In Meden Market? I doubt that.'

'But we don't know that the body came from Meden Market. It could have nothing whatever to do with Hugo or Russell Minty.'

She put out her tongue at me.

156

A minute later Susan hurried on to the terrace.

'It's Hugo,' she exclaimed breathlessly. 'He says he thought you might be here by now and he'd like a word with you.'

Talk of the devil — I followed her into the house and picked up the phone. Somewhere along the wire a woodpecker was beating a tattoo on a telegraph pole. I could hardly hear Hugo for a constant rattle in the earpiece.

'Hello, Alan!' He sounded merry and bright. 'Sorry to have missed you. What's all this about a nubile wench seeking audience with me? Sue said something about a cousin of yours. Is that right?'

'Yes. My cousin, Dorothy Merrack. Never mind. She'll survive the disappointment. Are you going to be in town for long?'

The woodpecker had been joined by a pneumatic drill and a percussion band. Hugo's voice was almost inaudible.

' . . . days. Not more. That's why I rang. Thought we might meet. Can I come over to your place?'

I thought quickly. This was all wrong. I

had no wish to have Hugo prowling round the vicinity of Baker Street. But at the same time I wanted that plot-book, and it seemed certain that I would only find it where Hugo was. If we arranged a meeting at my flat it was hardly likely that he would bring the book with him. I must get him to see me on his own ground.

'I'm a rolling stone these days, Hugo . . . ' He made some crack which was drowned by the appalling clatter on the line. ' . . . and I can't say when I'm likely to be at home this week. Couldn't we meet at your place? Where are you staying?'

' . . . Club . . . bit difficult. Better scrub round it this time, eh? Bring your cousin for a visit some weekend. We'll fix something up. Must dash now . . . publisher . . . Put Sue on again, will you?'

I handed the phone to Susan and strolled out into the garden. Dorothy looked up enquiringly.

'He doesn't sound like a man who's committed a murder,' I said.

★ ★ ★

Russell Minty's house wore a deserted air. A folded newspaper protruded from the letter-box and there was no reply to the pealing of the doorbell.

We were on the point of leaving when a cheerful voice hailed us from the garden.

'Looking for friend Minty?'

We turned and saw the Vicar strolling through the shrubbery with a twelve-bore under his arm. He crossed the drive and joined us on the doorstep.

'Off on his journeyings again, I'm afraid,' he said, nodding towards the house. 'Delightful chap, but erratic. Was he expecting you?'

'No. We called on the off-chance.' He exchanged introductions.

Bertrand Moss, Vicar of Meden Market, looked more soldier than parson.

'Rats,' he explained, brandishing the shotgun. 'Been at my chickens. The price of ovulation is constant vigilance. I mount a patrol most days. Bagged two or three in the last few weeks. Prefer a rifle, actually, but the police take a dim view of my old Lee-Enfield in open country.

Can't say I blame 'em. Deadly things. Come far?'

'From London.'

'Just on the off-chance? My hat, you can't know Minty very well. Care for a drink?'

In the welcome cool of the Vicarage drawing-room he faced us across a tiger-skin rug.

'Mind if I ask you a personal question?' he said as we sipped his excellent sherry.

'Go ahead.'

'Well, your visit intrigues me. I think I recognise you now. You're the Trevithick who got tangled up in the wheels of justice a couple of years back. A bad business, that. You were staying with the Mordants a few weeks ago.'

'You're well informed, Vicar.'

'Ha! My spies are everywhere! Gossip, y'know. Have to sort the wheat from the chaff, of course. Fact is, I was interested in your case at the time. Inspector Quill, wasn't it?'

I nodded.

'Thought so. Funny thing. Out in the garden this morning . . . saw a couple of chaps at Minty's front door. Turned out to be police. Quill, of all people. Should have thought this a bit off his patch. Wanted to know where Minty was. Couldn't tell 'em, of course. No idea myself. Thought about it a bit after they'd gone. *Quill*. Name rang a bell. Remembered your story in the Sunday papers. Quill — Trevithick. Association of ideas. Said to myself: 'Trevithick's been staying with the Mordants.' *Interesting*. Then . . . lo! You appear in the flesh, asking for Minty. Very popular chap, Minty, all of a sudden. None of my business, of course. But . . . *interesting*. Wouldn't you say?'

His assistance might be helpful. I told him everything.

He twirled his glass reflectively. 'So, Mrs Mordant's worried, eh? Understandable. But she's wrong about one thing. Minty came back after that first weekend.'

'You're sure?'

'Positive. Came in here on the Monday night to borrow some milk. Typical of the man. Never think of placing a regular order. Buys a bottle in the village when he needs it. Uses Marvel most of the time.

161

Must have run out.'

'Monday night. And he didn't say anything about going away again?'

'Nary a word. And he certainly didn't go off straight away. He was around on the Tuesday. Saw his lights on when I came across from the church after choir-practice. That would be about nine-thirty. Which reminds me. There was a Land Rover on the drive by his door.'

'Hugo Mordant has a Land Rover!'

'True. So does every farmer in the district — and umpteen other people, myself included. Very popular round here.'

'Have you any idea when the Land Rover left?'

The Vicar shook his head. 'We would have been in here watching television. I'm a shocking addict. And the drive doesn't pass these windows. Wait a minute, though. Yes, I remember. I did a late-night rat-patrol before turning in. That would be around half-eleven. The drive was empty then. Funny what you can remember when you set your mind to it.'

I thought back over the facts we had

collected during the last few hours. What else could the Vicar tell me? I asked about the duffle-coat. Would Minty have been wearing it?

The Reverend Mr Moss pondered my question. 'He certainly has a duffle-coat. Disgraceful old thing. Relic of his days with Air-Sea Rescue, I shouldn't wonder. But I don't think he'd wear it in this weather. He sports an anorak in summer if it rains. So, the body at the crem was arrayed in duffle, eh? And now we're all thinking the same thing. Well — ' He stood up. 'There's one way to find out. I have a key to Minty's place. In the circumstances I think we're justified in taking a peep inside.'

The artist's doormat was covered with newspapers and letters which jammed the door half-open as we entered. Slanting through the windows, the warm afternoon sun revealed a fine layer of dust on the polished furniture. We explored the whole house. One of the bedrooms had been converted into a studio and I recognised Susan's portrait on the easel. It was still unfinished. Downstairs in the hall a grandfather clock had ticked into silence days before, its hands arrested at ten past one. We had no idea what Minty had taken with him on his travels — except for one item. Thorough search revealed no duffle-coat on the premises.

'Well, that's something,' muttered the Vicar. We had spoken in whispers since crossing the threshold. 'But of course, it doesn't *prove* anything.'

Dorothy wandered into the tiny drawing-room and stood gazing round at the bachelor untidiness. Charred logs and powdered ash lay in the hearth. On a low table beside an armchair two tumblers and a whisky bottle nudged each other. Dust and fluff had formed a skin on the sticky drops in the bottom of each glass.

'You've been here before, Alan,' she said quietly. 'Is everything as it should be?'

I glanced about the room. 'As far as I can see. Of course, Sherlock would find half a dozen vital clues in here and the mystery would be solved — but we just don't know what we're looking for.'

The Vicar stooped to examine the

tumblers. 'Amateur's guess,' he said. 'But if he was entertaining someone, that Tuesday night, I'd say he cleared out before morning. Funny thing, y'know. No thought for his personal appearance, but very fastidious about the state of his home. But look at the furniture now — all over the place. And these dirty glasses. Ugh! Most unlike Minty. He must have left in a hurry.'

Back in the Vicarage, he filled an oversize calabash pipe with tobacco from a jar on the drawing-room mantelpiece.

'Grow my own,' he said proudly, ramming home the tangled amber shreds. He applied a match and puffed billowing grey clouds about the room. 'Potent stuff. Steep it in home-made brandy for a while. Fiendish! Nearly killed my curate. Sorts out the men from the boys! Care for a pipeful?' He picked up a virgin churchwarden clay from the mantelpiece and waved it at me through the thick haze. I shook my head and blinked the tears from my eyes.

'Wise man,' he said, and eased himself on to a forbidding Victorian sofa where he reclined at full length for a while, puffing away with an expression of pure bliss on his face. After some minutes he grunted and sat upright.

'This coffin business,' he said. 'Go over the details again, will you?'

I did a brief re-cap — throwing in my own theories for good measure. He nodded wisely at my suggestion that the bodies had been switched at the undertaker's.

'But not in that trumpery Chapel of Repose,' he said, emphatically. 'No. If old Chippy Teazle says that inner door was open, then it was open all right. Now, let's consider the facts carefully. I think we can take it that poor old Mary Porter was in the coffin when it arrived at the Chapel. Chippy Teazle says it wasn't tampered with while it was *in* the Chapel. And once they'd loaded it on to the hearse, it was in full view of somebody all the way to the crem. And there was no chance of any monkey business at the crem itself. Where does that leave us? Let me think . . . On the day of the funeral, what happened? We had Sir Henry Bonzell's funeral first

— at ten. That was a cremation, too. We were due at the crematorium at eleven. Now, wait a minute — it's coming back to me. They were busy at the crem that day, and Mary Porter's committal could only be fitted in at twelve-fifteen. That made it a bit of a rush. They drove me back to the church in the hearse — went at a fair old lick, too! The other cars were to drop off Sir Henry's mourners and go straight to Meden Vale to pick up the people for the Porter funeral. There weren't many. Just a few old folk and a couple of neighbours. The procession was back here at the church by twenty to twelve. The funeral was a straightforward affair. No hymns. We were on our way to the crem by twelve. Just made it nicely.'

A slight sound made me glance in Dorothy's direction. She was counting on her fingers and seemed to be working out some complicated mental arithmetic.

'Two hours,' she muttered. I touched her arm.

'Come back to us. What have you discovered?'

She looked up with triumph in her

eyes. 'Don't you see? If Sir Henry's funeral was at ten, I suppose they set off with the hearse at about nine-thirty to go to his house. Right?'

The Vicar nodded.

'Well then,' continued Dorothy, 'that means that from nine-thirty until, say, half past eleven, Mary Porter's coffin was left unattended in the Chapel of Repose.'

'Who says it was unattended?' I asked, unhelpfully.

'Ah, but she's right, y'know,' exclaimed the Vicar. 'Henderson is hard-up for bearers and drivers. It's a case of all hands to the pumps when he has a funeral. Yes, that coffin could have been left unattended for two hours. But . . . broad daylight? And Henderson's place is in the High Street. No. Somehow I can't see anyone breaking and entering at ten o'clock in the morning.'

Dorothy sighed. 'So, we're back to square one again. But just *supposing* another body had been put in that coffin, would the bearers have noticed any difference in weight when they lifted it into the hearse?'

'I doubt it,' said the Vicar. 'When four people are lifting something, it's difficult to judge its weight.'

I was still trying to fill out the picture of what happened on that Wednesday morning. The hearse would have come pelting back from Maunsley, through Meden Market and out to the parish church, which stood half-way between the village and the mining hamlet of Meden Vale. Time would be breathing down the necks of all involved in that funeral. After leaving the Vicar at his church gate, the hearse would be turned round and the bearers would speed back to Meden Market, a mile away, to pick up the coffin. The more I thought of that arrangement, the more ill-planned it seemed. Why waste so much precious time? They could have saved ten minutes or more by stopping at Henderson's place on the way to the church. Surely the Vicar would not have objected.

Dorothy's voice interrupted my train of thought.

'*Four* people? However many of you were there in that hearse? There's only one bench-type seat, isn't there? I should have thought three people at most.'

'That's right,' agreed the Vicar. 'Myself, old Chippy — he was driving — and a young chap from Meden Vale who helps out when he's on the right shift at the pit. I see what you mean. There were only two bearers. Still, I don't see what difference that makes. Anyway, if you want to know about the weight of that coffin you'd better ask them — though I doubt if they'd remember anything odd after all this time. They'll have handled a dozen coffins since then.'

'*I'd* like to ask them a question,' I said. 'Why didn't they stop to pick up the coffin when you passed through Meden Market on the way back from the crem? That would have saved time.'

The Vicar frowned. 'Why indeed? Funny you should mention that. I remember now . . . old Chippy seemed in no desperate hurry after he'd set me down at the church. Why, the old heathen even offered me a cigarette — just as if he had all the time in the world.'

'So much for Mr Henderson's image of

decorum and reverence,' said Dorothy. 'What an advertisement! An empty hearse stuck outside the church with two bearers smoking their heads off inside!'

'Oh, let's be fair,' exclaimed Moss. 'Even old Chippy wouldn't do that. We weren't exactly stuck outside the church in full view of the public gaze. He'd backed up the farm track beside the churchyard. I had to check that everything was in order up at the church, so I left him there, puffing away merrily. All very casual. I suppose he's got the routine worked out so well by now that funerals almost run themselves.'

I was still puzzled about the time factor.

'He'd have to get his skates on,' I said. 'How on earth did he manage it? Three minutes to Meden Market. Three minutes back again. Five minutes to load up. That's eleven minutes at the very least. And from what you've said, Vicar, I judge they only had fifteen minutes at the very outside. Four minutes to spare — and old Chippy settles down for a crafty drag as though he had all the time in the world.

171

That doesn't add up, somehow.'

'He'd know what he was about,' said the Vicar, confidently. 'I've never yet seen old Chippy in a flap. And the simple fact is that he was back in good time. When I walked down to the lych-gate about ten minutes later he'd got the hearse there, ready and waiting, long before the other cars came up from Meden Vale. You can ask him the secret of his success if you like, but it's hardly good form to expect a conjuror to reveal how he does his tricks.'

* ★ ★

Too many problems — that was my trouble. After dinner in the flat that evening I slipped out for a stroll in Regent's Park while Dorothy busied herself writing a sheaf of letters to her family announcing the glad tidings of our impending marriage. Girls like my cousin are expected to be blasé about such matters, bewailing matrimony as a fate worse than death — a pragmatic acceptance of outworn convention for the sake of the child whose conception has precipitated the crisis. If such be the rule, Dorothy was the exception. I left her busy with the fifth page of the fourth letter. She would be happily occupied for another couple of hours.

I was glad to be alone for a while. Too many problems . . . Already I was sick of the Russell Minty affair. It was a job for the police, not bungling amateurs. Until the previous night I could have enjoyed puzzling over the mystery surrounding Mary Porter's funeral. It would have been a welcome challenge. But now the most pressing problem was my forthcoming marriage, with its multitude of details to be settled. I was anxious to get down to Cornwall and make the necessary arrangements with the Rector of Listhowal. Compared with that, Russell Minty's disappearance was a triviality.

Then there was that wretched plot-book. I could not shrug that off without being disloyal to Inspector Quill. After all, I had offered to get it for him, and he was relying on me to rush in where he feared to tread.

But what more could I do? We had

tried . . . and failed. The book must be with Hugo, but where was he? Staying at the something-or-other Club. That was *most* helpful! Still — this was my problem. I shrank from the prospect of phoning every club in London to ask if he was there. Then I remembered *Who's Who*. Hugo was well enough up the literary ladder to merit a place in that register of success.

I walked homeward with a lighter step. First thing in the morning I would be round at the local reference library.

My confidence was unjustified. *Who's Who* listed three clubs against Hugo's name, and he was at none of them. But I was not to be beaten. I nipped into the fiction library and hunted along the shelves for his books. Between the works of Gabriel Morani and Elinor More there was a gaping void. Hugo must be very popular. I turned away and nearly collided with an assistant pushing a trolley containing books to be returned to the shelves. As I watched she lifted one volume, glanced at the index number and slammed it into the vacant space. *Gerona*

Steps — Hugo Mordant. I took it down and glanced at the title page. Published by Burroughs and Gwatkin. I scribbled the names in my diary.

Back in the flat, I phoned the publishers, giving my name and asking — as a friend of Hugo — where he might be found. The girl at the other end thought I wanted his home address and told me — politely but firmly — that such information could not be disclosed.

'That's O.K.,' I said. 'I know his Meden Market address, but I'm anxious to get hold of him today, while he's in London. I understand he was at your office yesterday, and I thought you might know where he's staying.'

After some delay I was put on to Edgar Gwatkin, who dealt with Hugo's work.

'I'm afraid I can't help you, Mr Trevithick. I haven't seen Hugo Mordant for ages. If you think he's in town, you might try the *Arts*.'

'Wasn't he at your place yesterday — or the day before?'

'I don't *think* so. Hold on — I'll check.' There was a long pause. In the background I could hear the clatter of a typewriter and the ringing of distant phone bells. Then Gwatkin came back on the line. 'No. I thought I wasn't mistaken. He hasn't been here.'

I thanked him and hung up. What was Hugo doing? Susan had been quite definite about the reason for his visit to London, and Hugo himself had mentioned his publisher over the phone.

I discussed this new development with Dorothy. She looked at me anxiously.

'D'you suppose he's been after *you*? After all, he wasn't to know you'd be going up to Meden Market. And that phone call just when you happened to be at his house . . . Why go to all that trouble on my account — a complete stranger? Was he checking up on your movements?'

'He did suggest that we all had dinner here.'

'Cheek! Look here, Alan, I'm prepared to admit my attractions, but surely that was far too gallant a gesture for an unknown fan. I bet he usually fobs people off with his autograph.'

'Hmm. I hadn't seen it that way.'

'You wouldn't,' she said brutally. But she was right. Hugo's anxiety to compensate Dorothy for her disappointment was out of proportion. He had obviously phoned for my special benefit, knowing that I would be at his house. Why? *Had* he come to London with the object of settling the score with me once and for all? I took a deep breath.

'Look, Dot,' I said. 'Aren't we letting our imagination run away with us? We're turning Hugo into a homicidal maniac. I'm convinced that he tried to do me in, three years ago. All right . . . maybe in a twisted way he thought he had good reason. And I'm sure he was all set to shove me off the church tower that Sunday afternoon. But what are we saying now? Hugo fails to dispose of me on Sunday afternoon, so he makes up for that disappointment by wiping out Russell Minty on the following Tuesday night; switches bodies — somehow — on Wednesday morning; dumps poor old Mary Porter in the North Sea . . . when? We don't know. Then — all within a matter of days — he's off to London and all set to finish me. That's piling it on a bit thick. Surely, if he'd murdered Minty and gone through all that caper with the coffin and the other body, he'd want to lie low for a bit. Blend with the scenery at Meden Market. Not come down here hell-bent on another killing which might point a finger straight at him. I'll need a good reason before I believe that.'

'O.K. I'll give you one,' said Dorothy evenly. 'But first — a question. Why did you think Susan Mordant was jumpy the other day?'

'You know the answer. Because I've a feeling she's looked inside that plot-book. So?'

'So we're back to the plot-book. Now, why are we interested in it? Because it gives the blue-print for the museum murder *and* because it may give us a clue to how and why Hugo set up that crazy double-shuffle with two bodies and one coffin. Right?'

I nodded.

'Right,' she said, warming to her subject. 'Now let's imagine Hugo suspects that you've read his precious book.

That's reasonable. You may have shown your suspicions. So he starts to wonder — after he's gone through with all that body-switching routine — if you've opened his Pandora's Box and read his guilty secret. See what that means? The moment he thinks that, you're no longer just his wife's lover of three years back . . . you're the one man who can blow his perfect crime wide open. So what does he do? He grabs the plot-book and comes down here to rub you out. Don't ask me how he plans to do it, but I'll bet he's got half a dozen assorted schemes worked out in that book of his.'

'Go on,' I said. 'All this is pure speculation. How about a few facts?'

'I haven't any. My guess is he came here the day before yesterday, after we'd set out for Meden Market. I'd say he came in the afternoon. Yes, that fits. He came in the afternoon, found you'd gone, and then — realising it was going to be a longer job than he'd expected — he phoned his wife to say he wouldn't be back for a day or two. Then she told him about our visit, so he phoned again the next day, knowing you'd be at his house, and tried to fix a meeting with you. How's that?'

'Very clever,' I said loftily. 'Now we'll just cut it down to size.'

I picked up the house-phone and spoke to the porter on the ground floor.

'Anyone call while I was away?' I made faces at Dorothy as I spoke. My superior smirk vanished abruptly at his reply.

'There was a gent here the other day, sir. I didn't think it worth telling you. He said he'd be back.'

'You've no idea who it was, I suppose?'

'Sorry, Mr Trevithick. Never seen him before. I sort of got the idea he was from up north. When I told him you'd just left for Meden Market he said, 'Dammit, we must have passed each other.' He wouldn't leave no message. Said he'd be back.'

That was enough for me. I turned to Dorothy.

'Start packing. We're off to Cornwall straight away.'

8

For six idyllic days we forgot Hugo Mordant, Russell Minty, Mary Porter, Chippy Teazle, Old Uncle Tom Cobley and all. The only cloud on my horizon — and that had a silver lining — was the knowledge that our marriage would not be accomplished as speedily as I wished. Dorothy decided on a white wedding after all, and that meant invitations, bridesmaids, buffet reception . . . the lot.

We swore the necessary affidavit and the licence was issued within a few days. We could now be married in Listhowal Church any time in the next three months, so we settled for the first Saturday in August. The wording of that licence fascinated me, with its flamboyant greeting from the Bishop's Vicar General. He couldn't know me from Adam, yet he hailed me as 'Our Well Beloved In Christ Alan Michael Trevithick' and wished me Grace and Health.

'Whereas', he proclaimed, '*ye are, as it is alleged, resolved to proceed to the Solemnization of true and lawful Matrimony and that you greatly desire that the same be solemnized in the face of the Church: WE being willing that these your honest Desires may the more speedily obtain a due effect . . . graciously GRANT this our LICENCE AND FACULTY . . .* '

It took him a full sheet of foolscap to do just that. But it was worth it.

Then, suddenly, the holiday was over. The postman brought a laconic note from Inspector Quill.

'*Have you retired?*'

I guessed what disappointment lay behind that question. In relying on me he had leaned on the proverbial broken reed. At least I owed him an explanation. Our departure from London had been in the nature of headlong flight. We could not avoid Hugo indefinitely. By now he must have returned to Meden Market. We should be safe enough in the flat — if we were careful.

I planned to leave Dorothy in Listhowal

and return to London alone.

'Not on your life,' she said. 'I'm not letting you out of my sight.'

Force majeure.

We set off one glorious morning, driving slowly along deep lanes between hedges aflame with blossom.

In the village a constable halted us with an imperious hand. The narrow road past the church was blocked by sedate Rolls-Royces drawn up behind an empty hearse. Down the path from the old grey building came the bearers, trundling the coffin on a folding metal trolley which robbed the procession of all dignity. They might have been pushing a pram or a supermarket trolley. By the lych-gate they opened the rear door of the hearse, lifted the coffin from the trolley, slid it gently into the venerable Rolls and fixed it securely in position. One of the men folded the trolley, opened a lower door and hid the inelegant thing in a large storage compartment. With practised skill the undertaker shepherded the mourners into the waiting cars. They shuffled past the hearse, some casting sidelong glances at the coffin behind the bevelled windows, while others stared stolidly ahead as though refusing to acknowledge its presence. The coffin itself was a plain affair. In place of the brass knobs of the old music-hall ditty there were simple wooden pegs, while the handles were no more than short lengths of rope with wooden toggles.

'Poverty-stricken,' I muttered. Dorothy followed my gaze.

'Practical,' she said. 'It's going to be burned in half an hour.'

In just such a coffin had Mary Porter's body set out on its journey, only to be ousted before it reached the refining fire.

We watched the cortège move slowly away. The constable waved us on, and we continued what was to be an uneventful journey to Baker Street.

The apparently trivial episode must have registered deeply in my unconscious. That night I dreamed about it. Nothing unpleasant or horrific. More a videotape recording, with every detail clear. In the morning it still lingered on the retina of my mind.

Then — in a dazzling flash of intuition — the truth dawned.

We had finished breakfast and I was about to make my peace with Quill. I had even lifted the phone from its cradle and begun to dial the number when revelation hit me. I stood there, my finger in one of the holes in the dial and the receiver making odd noises in my ear.

'Eureka!' I did not shout aloud like triumphant Archimedes. The words came out in a whisper. Then I clapped the phone back on its rest and hurried in search of Dorothy.

She was stacking crockery into the service lift. I leaned against the wall at her side and said, as nonchalantly as I could, 'One problem solved.'

'Oh yes?' She turned away to collect our cups from the table. I tried again.

'I know how the conjuring trick was done.'

She placed another load in the lift, closed the door and pressed the operating button. Then she turned and faced me.

'Now,' she said, like a patient mother with a persistent child. 'What are we supposed to be talking about? Which conjuring trick?'

I felt deflated. 'Chippy Teazle's,' I said. The name sounded more ridiculous than usual. At last she looked interested.

'Ah. You mean how he managed to get to Meden Market and back in record time.'

That's just it. '*He didn't.*'

'Come again?'

'He didn't go to Meden Market. Remember that funeral yesterday morning? That, my girl, was as good a clue as we're ever likely to get. Think back. What did they do with that trolley?'

She closed her eyes. 'They wheeled it down the path . . . folded it up . . . and shoved it in that cupboard place at the back of the hearse.' She opened her eyes and smiled at me. 'Right?'

'Full marks. But that cupboard place, as you call it, was . . . how big?'

'Oh, goodness, I haven't a clue. About the size of a car boot? I couldn't see from where I was sitting.'

'Ah, but *I could*. That compartment stretched right under where the coffin

186

was resting. Does that suggest anything to you?'

'Frankly, no.'

I pushed myself away from the wall. 'Oh, for heaven's sake . . . *look* . . . ' Snatching an envelope from the table, I drew a rough sketch. 'There. One hearse. Now, that's where the coffin rests, see? There, I'll put a coffin in . . . brass knobs and all. But do you see what I see, cousin? *There's room for another coffin underneath!*' I held up the sketch for her inspection.

'Of course!' she breathed. 'It's so simple when you know how. Old Chippy had Mary Porter's coffin tucked away underneath Sir Henry's all the time! The crafty old devil! No wonder he could afford time off for a smoke. And I suppose they backed the hearse up that farm track so they could get her out from below and put her on the top deck without anyone seeing what was happening.'

'Only it wasn't *her*. It was X — the unidentified body which has now been dissipated to the four winds.'

'Russell Minty,' she said doggedly.

'Have it your own way. I won't argue. But d'you see what this means? That coffin was not left unattended during Sir Henry's funeral. So . . . the bodies *must* have been switched between the time old Chippy packed up for the night on Tuesday, and the time he clocked on again on Wednesday morning.'

'While the coffin was in the Chapel of Thingamyjig? What about the alarm bell? 'Guaranteed to wake the dead, sir, if you'll excuse my little joke' — and all that jazz.'

I bit my lip. I'd forgotten that bell. 'Maybe it wasn't switched on that night.'

Dorothy dismissed the idea with a wave of her hand. 'You heard old Chippy. '*Ar!*' he said, and '*Ar!*' he meant. *Faithful Unto Death* must be his motto. You're suggesting that he just happened to forget that alarm bell on the very night someone decided to pinch a corpse. Even Inspector Quill wouldn't swallow that much coincidence.'

'Then . . . how?'

For half a minute I stood there,

puzzling over the mechanics of the problem. Then — suddenly — I knew I'd had enough. Enough of Quill and Hugo and coffins and all the rest. The time for academic discussion was past. If I was to get that load of mischief off my back, I must act decisively — rashly if necessary — and without more delay. The heart of the mystery was in Meden Market, so to Meden Market I would go.

Without another word, I strode to the phone and got the Mordants' number. Susan answered. I asked for Hugo. There was a pause while she went in search of him. After a couple of minutes she was back.

'He's in the bath, Alan? Is it important? He'll ring you back, if you like.'

I told her not to bother . . . I'd be getting in touch later. We chatted about nothing for another minute and then hung up. Good. Hugo was at home. The plot-book must be there now. I turned to Dorothy.

'Want to be a burglar? I've had enough play-acting. Tonight I'm going to get that book, if I have to ransack every room in Hugo's house.'

Her eyes were shining. 'I'm on.'

* ★ ★

At two o'clock that night I parked the Capri in a side street fifty yards from Henderson's funeral parlour. The moon was full, and by its light I could see Dorothy's puzzled frown as we stood on the pavement.

'I thought we were going to Hugo's,' she whispered.

'Later. First we'll see what's so special about that Chapel of Repose. There *must* be a way in. If Hugo could find it, so can I.'

We were dressed for the occasion in dark-blue anoraks. Dorothy wore black stretch-pants, and we were both shod with rubber soles.

Leaving the car, we kept to the shadows in front of Henderson's office and turned up the alley leading past the side door. No windows broke the blank wall on each side of the Chapel entrance. An intruder must force that door or remain outside.

The bright moon glowed on the varnished panels and struck sparks from the metal handles. At one glance I saw how hollow was my boast of finding a way in. An expert might have picked the lock, but I knew nothing of such skills.

Dorothy touched my arm and pointed upwards. High on an inaccessible gable end, the large alarm bell mocked us in the moonlight. There was no point in standing around any longer. I led the way further along the alley. After a few yards it turned the corner of the building and opened on to a courtyard flanked by garages. Beyond, two wooden gates barred the way. I eased back one — it wasn't locked — and peered cautiously through the opening.

On the far side lay a narrow road, parallel with the High Street. It was a cul-de-sac, blocked at one end by railings beyond which I glimpsed bright water — the local canal. At its other end, the road formed a T-junction with a broader thoroughfare leading back towards the High Street. The cul-de-sac had the desolate air of a war-ravaged city. Piles of rubble marked the sites of half a dozen houses. Those still standing were empty. Already the bulldozers had gnawed at a derelict pub, leaving it little more than a shell. The side wall had gone and the moon lighted the bar window, throwing into silhouette the stencilled word SNUG. The effect was uncanny. I caught myself listening for the tinkle of a ghostly piano.

Closing the gate, I turned back to the garages. They housed the small fleet of Rolls-Royces which comprised Henderson's funeral convoy. I could just make out the cars through the windows in the side of each garage. All the buildings were locked, except one — and that contained the hearse. Perhaps the undertaker reasoned that nobody would risk stealing so outlandish a vehicle.

I handed Dorothy my torch.

'If this thing is open, I'll show you what I mean about that bottom compartment,' I whispered.

The handle of the lower door moved noiselessly and we found ourselves looking into the dark recess of the storage space. Taking the torch, I flashed it round the interior of the vehicle. Dorothy gasped.

On the floor of that lower compartment was a coffin.

★   ★   ★

I snapped out the light.

'All ready for tomorrow's performance,' I murmured. 'Another one of Chippy's conjuring tricks. D'you suppose he makes a regular practice of this?'

Dorothy glanced round the moonlit courtyard. 'This is where it happened,' she said quietly. 'It's the obvious place. You can't be overlooked. As long as you're quiet, you can take as long as you like over the job. See . . . you can drive a car right up to those gates, carry a body in here, swap it for the one in the coffin, and away you go.'

'Hang on,' I muttered. 'Let's check this thing. I want to see what the screws are like.' I seized one of the handles and dragged the coffin half out of the hearse. Dorothy shone the torch, masking the light carefully.

The lid was fastened with ordinary wood screws. To remove it would have taken no more than five minutes with a screwdriver.

Carefully, we restored everything to its rightful place and crept stealthily back to the car. A cigarette was more than welcome.

'There's still a snag,' I said. 'We've seen how the trick was done, but how on earth did Hugo know there'd be a body tucked away in that hearse on the very night he made away with Minty?'

'You agree it *was* Minty?'

I nodded. 'It couldn't very well be anyone else. But how did Hugo *know*?'

She drew on her cigarette thoughtfully. 'Hmm. He could hardly ring up Henderson and say, 'Look here, old chap, I want to commit a murder tonight. Any chance of a spare body?' Yet he must have known somehow. The whole thing had to be worked out to the last detail. He could have been planning it for weeks — months. And it all depended on another body being available in the right place at the right time. D'you suppose it *had* to be

194

a body intended for cremation? Or was that just a fluke? If so, it was a damned lucky one for him. No chance of exhumation.'

I tried to look at things from Hugo's angle. That second body was essential. He could not risk the murder without it . . . and there it was, all ready and waiting on the night he'd chosen for his crime.

Of course! I turned eagerly to Dorothy. 'We've got things back to front. Hugo wasn't a clairvoyant — and he didn't trust to luck. Somehow he'd found out that once in a while there was a coffin left here overnight. Maybe at first that only gave him an idea for a story. Then he decided to use his knowledge in a scheme to get rid of Minty. But he kept the arrangements fluid. Whatever plan he had was the sort that can be put into action at very short notice. And he only set the ball rolling when he knew for certain that there was another body available. How did he find that out? The same way we did — by coming down here to look. His luck may have been out half a dozen times, but the night he found Mary

Porter's coffin in the hearse, Minty was doomed. Cremation was part of the plan. No incriminating evidence afterwards. And you can tell from the type of coffin used whether or not a body is to be cremated. You pointed that out to me the other day.'

Dorothy stared ahead through the windscreen. 'Sitting here, that all sounds completely reasonable. We've seen the hearse and the coffin. We could have done the whole thing ourselves and nobody any the wiser. But I'd hate the job of convincing a jury. They'd think it fantastic.'

I turned the ignition key.

'Come on,' I said grimly. 'Let's get that book.'

* * *

We left the car on the farm track by the church and walked a couple of hundred yards to the end of Hugo's drive. Standing in the dappled shadows of some young lime trees, we made our final plans.

'How do we get in?' whispered Dorothy.

I stood and placed my lips close to her ear. 'We don't. I'm going in alone.'

'But . . . '

I cut short her protest. 'It's only common sense. I know the geography of the house — and one of us must stay outside to keep watch and create a diversion if anything goes wrong.'

'How?'

'Make as much racket as possible. Kick over the dustbin; heave a stone through a window; anything to give me a chance to get away. And don't hang around. If anything goes wrong, I'll give a shout. You start diverting like mad and then scoot.'

'What if somebody chases me?'

'Don't sound so hopeful,' I hissed. 'Make for the car and get away. Here's the key. Don't put the lights on till you're way down the road. We don't want our number spotted. If you can't reach the car in time, *hide*.'

'You think of everything, coz.'

'I'm trying to — but this isn't my cup of tea.'

'How about you — if anything goes wrong?'

I squeezed her arm. 'I'll fade into the night like the wily Bedouin and see you back at the flat, sometime.'

My plan was to try the easiest way in first. The back door might be unlocked. I'd defaulted in that respect often enough at the Oxted house. Failing that, I would try the french windows of Hugo's study, and, if that proved useless, it would have to be one of the downstairs windows. The best bet was the kitchen or the cloak-room. My amateur burglar's kit was crude in the extreme. A couple of screwdrivers, a chisel and an old Scout knife. Without expertise, brute force and ignorance must needs carry the day.

We crept along the drive and past the old coach-house which served as a garage. The doors stood open, and I could see the Land Rover and Hugo's green M.G. Such indifference to security raised hopes of easy access to the house. Thank God there was no dog on the premises.

Confidence began to ebb when we

found the back door and the french windows secured. Both were beyond my ability as a thief in the night. The kitchen window was a modern affair with a steer frame, but . . . just as desperation was boiling up within me . . . we found the cloakroom window partly open.

So far I had done nothing unlawful, yet the tension was such that my nylon shirt was already soaked with sweat and clinging to my body. Hardly daring to breathe, I inched the window up until there was room enough to scramble through. Dorothy touched my sleeve.

'Want a bunk-up?'

I nodded. Beneath the window a waste-pipe stuck out from the wall. I placed one foot on it and grasped the window frame with both hands. Dorothy crouched and put her shoulder under my seat.

'*Now!*' I whispered, and heaved myself up. The thrust of her shoulder threw me across the ledge with such force that the breath was knocked out of me. As I lay gasping, half in and half out of the room, I felt her grip my legs and push me further forward. My gloved hands groped in the darkness and found the rim of the wash-basin. Another shove from below and my knees were on the ledge. The next minute my feet were on the cloakroom floor, and I leaned out of the window to give final instructions to my partner in crime.

'Go round to the french windows and wait. I'll come out that way. If I shout, make a hell of a din and *run*. O.K.?'

'Will do. Alan — *be careful*. Don't forget, he's dangerous.'

Her warning was superfluous.

Without a sound, I opened the cloakroom door and listened. The house was silent. As I stole along the carpeted passage, the grandfather clock gave an almighty *thump!* — whirred, rattled — and struck three. My taut abdomen pleaded for relief — an unforeseen complication. Dismissing its appeal, I tiptoed across the hall.

In Hugo's study the curtains were closed, the room dark as the pit. I fished the torch from my pocket and pressed the button. Nothing happened. *What the hell . . . ?* Something loose? I twisted the end of the case and tried again. No joy. The bulb must have come unscrewed. My driving gloves made the job impossible. As I fumbled to remove them I felt the torch slip from my grasp. For one age-long second I stood there, rigid with suspense. Somewhere by my feet the carpet cushioned the impact. My gasp of relief sounded like a wave breaking on shingle.

I groped eagerly — fool that I was — sending the metal case clattering across the parquet floor.

For a full minute I did not dare to move. Sixty seconds in which I was made aware, in rapid succession, of a dry mouth, thumping heart, trembling legs . . . and that half-thermos of coffee I had imprudently swallowed three hours earlier.

Already my sense of direction was confused. Finding the torch might mean five minutes blundering into furniture, sending ornaments flying and waking Hugo and Susan in the room above. I decided to risk the electric light. The study door closed quietly enough, but the Literary Lion favoured fluorescent lighting, and by pressing the switch I loosed a minor electric storm above my head. The flashes and pops gave way to a steady hum, as though a hive of bees had been disturbed.

I scooped my wayward torch from the floor and examined it. Useless . . . the bulb was broken. The top drawer of Hugo's desk was locked. Forcing my hefty screwdriver into the crack above the keyhole, I levered upwards — to be rewarded by the sound of metal snapping. In another second the drawer was open — but there was no book. Hopefully I eased the drawer right out of the desk. It was not completely empty. Right at the back lay an automatic — twin to the one that had sent Milo Hagerty on his last journey. Self-preservation is a powerful instinct. I pocketed the weapon. You never know . . .

Where would Hugo hide that book? I wasted ten minutes hunting along his shelves. Then I saw it. *What Men Know About Women*. While I was breaking into the desk, that precious volume had been within a foot of my hand, bang in the middle of the blotting-pad. What was the catch? There lay *Exhibit A* in all its glory — as if Hugo wanted it found. That was too subtle for me. Maybe I was swallowing a hook. I unzipped my anorak and slid the book inside. Tiptoeing to the door, I switched out the light.

Accustomed to the subdued hum from the fluorescent tubes, my hearing seemed suddenly more acute in the unnatural quiet of the dark room. I began to walk slowly towards the french windows, but before I had taken four paces a slight noise brought me to a halt, poised like a ballet-dancer in an action photo.

Someone was opening the door.

I turned, straining my eyes to glimpse a silhouette against the moonlight in the hall. That was my undoing. From above my head came a slight *pop!* Even as I glanced up, instinctively, the fluorescent tube sprang to life. Dazzled, I was helpless against my assailant. Something hard slammed against the side of my head, knocking me sideways across the desk. I remember thinking — with complete detachment — *'How long before I pass out?* Then I was rushing headlong into a noisy tunnel of oblivion.

But in that brief space between the blow and unconsciousness I heard a woman's voice.

'It's Alan!'

9

Susan was bathing my head with a wet towel as I lay on the study floor. How long had I been unconscious? Long enough to be involved in a complicated dream with Hugo as a sinister Roman Tribune menacing me with a vicious *pilum* which he was intent on thrusting into my stomach. I stared stupidly up at Susan.

*Susan . . . Meden Market . . . Hugo's study . . . .*The elements of the situation began to register.

She knelt over me, her dark hair falling forward and brushing my cheek as she gazed anxiously into my face.

'Are you all right, Alan?' Her voice seemed locked up in a distant echo-chamber. I tried to nod. It was all wrong that she should be concerned for my welfare when I had been caught in the act of burgling her house. Before I could reply there was a sound of footsteps in the hall and Dorothy burst into the room, her eyes blazing.

'What in God's name are you doing?' she demanded, thrusting Susan aside and kneeling beside me. My face was cupped in her warm hands, and for a brief moment I experienced a blessed sense of safety. Then I remembered.

'Hugo!' I struggled to rise, but she held me back.

'He's gone.'

'*Gone?*' When he had me at his mercy?

'I heard him run out of the back door. Thought it was you, so I nipped round there just in time to see him making off in the Land Rover.'

I looked helplessly at Susan. 'I'm sorry about this, Sue.'

She seemed remarkably composed. 'It had to come. I've been expecting it for ages.'

'You know then ... about what happened at the museum that night?'

She nodded miserably. 'I read how he did it . . . in that book of his. But he killed the wrong man, didn't he?'

I got slowly to my feet and felt the side

of my head gingerly.

'He did. So you can guess why I'm here.' I pulled the plot-book from my anorak. 'Sue, I'm sorry — but the police must have this. You do realise that, don't you? It's not just because of Milo Hagerty. You've read this book. Can't you see what else has happened?'

She stared at me blankly. There was no easy way to break it to her.

'Russell Minty,' I said gently.

'Oh, *no!*' The news must have been a blow, yet again I wondered at her composure. I opened the book.

'We know how he did it — at least, we know how he got rid of Minty's body. Let's just check.' I flicked over the pages. 'Here we are . . .'

Hugo's notes — brief, almost incoherent — confirmed our suspicions.

'*Crematorium. Ashes pulverised. No identifiable remains. Second coffin overnight in hearse. No brass fittings if for crem. Need screwdriver. Mirror. Weight body. Check currents. Disfigure second body.*'

Hugo's thoughts, jerked on to paper in cryptic shorthand, were clear to me — and that last sentence disturbed me more than the rest. A cold-blooded act in every sense.

I looked up at Susan. 'Minty's dead and his ashes scattered. But the police have another body which should have been cremated at Maunsley — and there are witnesses to prove that a body *was* cremated. Even if we can't prove it was Minty, we still have this book as evidence that Hugo was involved.'

I expected her to plead Hugo's friendship and beg my help in clearing him, but she had no illusions.

'How blind you must have thought me, Alan.'

'But you'd guessed the truth, even before Dorothy and I called here last week. I could tell.'

She nodded. 'I didn't know what to do. These last few weeks have been a nightmare.'

'What made you look in this book? It's been lying around for years. Why the sudden interest?'

'That was you again. Russell Minty told me you'd been to see him — and what you said. So when you came that weekend I watched you carefully. That Saturday night I heard you go down to Hugo's study and I followed you.'

'Without Hugo's knowledge?'

'He was asleep.' She spoke confidently. 'I saw you looking at that book. There was no sense in my hanging around just then, but, as soon as I could, I read it for myself. That was while you were out, that Sunday afternoon. Oh, *Lord!*' She sank wearily into an armchair. 'What are we going to do, Alan?'

I pushed the book back inside my anorak. 'We'll phone the police. Not the local crowd. That would mean too much explaining. I'll get on to Inspector Quill straight away.'

'At this time of night?' As though to emphasise Susan's words, the grandfather clock struck the half-hour. Was it only thirty minutes since its chimes had stopped me in my tracks out in the hall? Quill would be one of the gentlemen in England now abed. There was no point

209

in phoning his office until around nine. Six hours. In that time I could be in London, handing over my precious evidence in person.

Dorothy read my thoughts. 'If you're thinking of going to London, Alan, forget it. Quill's got to come up here anyway — and we can't very well leave Susan on her own now.'

Susan waved away the suggestion. 'I'll be all right. I'm not afraid of staying here alone.'

'That's not the point,' persisted Dorothy. 'Hugo's on the loose. He could come back here any time. Especially as he must know you suspect him, Susan.'

'But why should he think that? I've been most careful . . . '

'Maybe. But he knows he clobbered Alan — and what more natural than Al should tell you why he's here? Hugo must know what's behind this midnight call.'

I nodded. 'He knows I'm on to the truth about Milo's death. I'm not much of an actor. *And* he can't think I'm so dim that I don't realise he tried to push me off the church tower.'

'*Here?*' Clearly this was news to Susan.

'That same weekend. But we're not doing any good standing about like spare parts.'

'I'll get some coffee' — Susan's conditioned reflex. I shook my head, and immediately regretted the action.

'Not for me. I'm all in — and my head's playing up. If I don't get some sleep I'll be fit for nothing in the morning.'

Immediately she was full of concern. 'What am I thinking of? You must have the guest room.' She glanced from me to Dorothy. 'Are you sleeping together?' she asked.

My cousin and I answered at the same moment.

'No!' I said.

'*Yes!*' Dorothy said it again for good measure. 'Yes.'

I was annoyed — with Susan for asking in the tone reserved for such mundane questions as 'One lump or two?' — and with Dorothy for . . . well, I wasn't quite sure what.

Susan shrugged her shoulders. 'Well,

when you've made up your minds, there are two beds in the spare room — or a studio couch in here.'

'The bedroom,' said Dorothy, emphatically. She turned to me. 'D'you think he'll come back?'

'Hugo? I doubt it. He missed his opportunity just now. If he comes back, he'll have to deal with all of us — and that's not easy. For all he knows, we may have called the police. No. I think we can count on a few hours' sleep.'

'What about the car?' asked Dorothy. 'Will it be safe?'

'I'm past caring.'

Fifteen minutes later, having checked that the house was secure, we were upstairs, getting ready for bed. Dorothy and I were kitted out with borrowed nightdress and pyjamas. My distaste at the thought of wearing Hugo's things was overcome by my craving for sleep.

'Separate beds,' said Dorothy when we were alone. 'I only suggested this lark so we'd be together. We mustn't split forces at this stage. And whether you like it or not, I'll undress in the dark. I'm not rousing your animal passions in these compromising circumstances.'

The next moment the room was in darkness.

Just as I was dropping off, she said softly, 'Susan's taking all this very calmly. Sort of fatalistic. Did you notice?'

'Go to sleep.'

'Sorry!'

It seemed only a moment later that she was shaking me awake in a room full of sunlight with the sounds of the countryside drifting through the open window.

'Alan! Wake up!'

'What? . . . Where? . . . ' Memory of the night's events came flooding back. 'Grief! What time is it?'

'It's after ten. We've both overslept — and *she's gone!*'

'Susan? Gone?'

'Yes. I went along to the bathroom and her door was open. The bedroom's empty and there's no sign of her downstairs. The other car's gone, too. I checked.'

'Shopping?'

She shook her head impatiently. 'Don't you see? *She's gone after Hugo!*'

Mid-day. We were demolishing a hefty brunch which Dorothy had whipped up in Susan's American-style kitchen. I had phoned Quill, fetched the Capri and soaked away the night's exertions in a hot bath. There was nothing else for us to do. The hour of the amateur was past. Quill was on his way, fuming at our incompetence, having initiated a nationwide search for the Land Rover and the M.G. Our failure even to note their numbers had called down his wrath on our penitent heads.

'I feel a complete clown,' said Dorothy. 'Quill treats us both like kids. Matter of fact, I thought we'd done rather well for him. Hang it — this was his idea. He practically went down on his knees for this plot-book.'

I attacked my eggs and bacon. 'You won't get him to admit that,' I told her between mouthfuls. 'If he hasn't blown a fuse before he gets here, he'll pull us in for breaking and entering.'

I was wrong. Quill arrived in good

humour. He was even apologetic.

'Sorry about the broadside over the phone,' he said affably. 'I'm so used to dealing with professionals that I forget myself at times. Let's have a gander at this famous book.'

He studied *What Men Know About Women* for ten minutes. At last he put it down and stood for a few moments, whistling softly between his teeth.

'I'm convinced,' he said. 'But will this be any good in court without hard facts to support it?'

We recounted our exploits of the previous night.

'Damn Henderson!' he muttered angrily. 'Why couldn't he have told us about that second coffin routine?'

'Bad for his image,' suggested Dorothy. 'And he may not have known. It could be one of Chippy Teazle's little trade secrets. What puzzles me is how Hugo Mordant found out.'

'I think I know,' I said. 'Look at those notes in his book. He's obviously written them at different times. Now the first entry is about cremation. I'd say he began

215

by collecting material for a novel which was to centre on a cremation. That would make him find out what leads up to cremation. He probably nosed around Henderson's place on the quiet and spotted someone stowing a coffin into the hearse one evening. He'd work out the rest for himself.'

Quill studied the notes again. 'He'd need a screwdriver and a mirror,' he said slowly. 'Why?'

'Simple,' I said loftily. 'Screwdriver to open the coffin and screw it down again after he'd switched corpses. And I suppose he'd use the mirror to check that his victim was really dead. You know — holding it near his mouth to see if he was breathing — as per the first-aid manual.'

'Could be.' Quill sounded unconvinced. '*Check currents*. Now that's interesting. Old Mary Porter was picked up some miles off shore, and the coastguard people reckon she was on her way back to land. In other words, she must have been pitched overboard well out to sea.'

'Weighted?' asked Dorothy. 'Hugo makes a point of that.'

Quill nodded. 'Almost certainly weighted. But Mordant was no fool. He would have known that even a weighted body can move if the current's strong enough. And there's always the chance that it might break adrift from its moorings. He had to make sure that if either of those things happened, the body wouldn't turn up until it was virtually unrecognisable. And that's just what he did. Poor old Mary was a sheer hulk by the time she was dredged up. That wedding ring was a thousand-to-one chance. We'd never have identified her otherwise.'

'Did he . . . ' Dorothy hesitated. 'Did he disfigure the face?'

Quill shrugged. 'Didn't look like it. Not that there was much face left — but there was no bone damage — as there would have been if he'd bashed it in. But how the devil did he manage to get the body so far out to sea in the first place?'

I snatched the book excitedly.

'It's staring us in the face. *Mirror*. Hugo bought a Mirror Offshore yacht last year. That's what he means here. He used the boat to move the body. Of course — it all fits. The canal runs past the end of the street behind Henderson's garages. And all the houses are empty. No one would have seen him.'

Quill chewed his lower lip thoughtfully. 'Let's work it out,' he said.

Hugo's study yielded not only a good road atlas, but also a battered and stained copy of Stanford's map of the inland waterways of Britain.

We started with the assumption that Minty was killed on the Tuesday night before the funeral, and that the Land Rover seen by the Vicar was Hugo's. As we pictured it, Minty's body was loaded into the Land Rover and driven to the back of Henderson's premises. There the bodies were switched and Mary Porter's corpse was driven the couple of hundred yards to the canal where the Mirror Offshore would have been moored. The rest seemed easy. The canal flowed into the Trent, the Trent into the Humber — and the Humber into the North Sea. I traced the route with my finger.

'There,' I said proudly, tapping the blue expanse east of Grimsby. 'How's that for a reconstruction of the crime?'

For some moments Quill sat in silence, poring over the map. Then he looked up.

'It won't do,' he said simply.

'But it's so obvious.' I was peeved at his lack of enthusiasm.

'To you, maybe. But then, you're no yachtsman, are you?'

'No. But so what?'

He pointed to the map again. 'So this. You can't rush around on rivers and canals like you can on roads. What you're suggesting is that Mordant took his craft down the canal, through the lock, down the Trent to Trent Falls, and along the Humber, single-handed and at night. And at no more than five miles an hour — don't forget that. I'm not saying it can't be done, but it's damned tricky — especially the Humber. Then he comes all the way back. That's a full day's trip — and if he didn't want to be spotted in daylight it would have taken him even longer, hanging about waiting for dark. What is he — a master mariner?'

'No — just a weekend sailor. He was in Naval Intelligence at one time,' I added helpfully. Quill snorted.

'Polishing his backside in Whitehall, most likely. Naval Intelligence is no apprenticeship for handling a small craft on a river like the Humber. Still — it's an interesting point. Gives us a little more insight into his mind. He may know *something* about the sea. Look — I'm with you some of the way. What you suggest about switching the bodies — that's reasonable. But if he did use the boat — what did he do with the Land Rover once the body was aboard?'

I had no answer for that. If Hugo had been away for as long as Quill suggested, would he have risked leaving the Land Rover parked by the canal? The workmen demolishing the houses in that street would see it — and if it was there for long, they might become suspicious and notify the police.

Quill stood up. 'We're talking in the dark,' he said. 'Let's have a look at that boat.'

We drove to the yacht basin in the

police car. Hugo's white-hulled Mirror Offshore lay moored at a distance from the other craft. The place was deserted. Obviously the other boat-owners were also weekend skippers.

Below decks — if so grandiloquent an expression is appropriate for so small a ship — chaos reigned. The cabin floor was littered with cans of food — most of them without labels. On one bunk lay a chart of the North Sea and an R.A.C. Handbook. Mildew blossomed on the bedding, and the place reeked with damp.

Quill hissed with disapproval.

'What a shambles! There's no need for a craft like this to get into such a state. It's a damned disgrace. People shouldn't buy yachts unless they know how to look after 'em.'

He stooped and tugged at a piece of white material caught on the latch of the cabin door.

'Aha!' he murmured. 'Know what this is?'

Dorothy handled the soiled fragment carefully.

'Looks like part of a wedding dress,'

she said, uncertainly.

Quill was enjoying himself. 'No.' He chuckled. 'Just the opposite. I saw this sort of stuff only the other day — in Henderson's funeral emporium. Can't mistake it. *It's part of a shroud.* So that answers one of our questions. He had the body aboard. And I'll tell you something else.' He sniffed. 'This cabin stinks of salt water. I'll wager this boat's been to sea recently. Mordant must be a better sailor than I thought. Let's see if anyone round here noticed the boat was missing on the day of the funeral.'

We were in luck. The local pub overlooked the basin, and the landlord regarded himself as unofficial guardian of the craft.

'Good customers, them owners,' he explained. 'Least I can do is keep an eye on their property. We had a spot of pilfering, back around Easter time. Outboards, mostly . . . and one or two boats lost compasses and odd bits of gadgets. I usually takes a stroll 'long the waterside last thing . . . and sometimes of a daytime I'll just take a look-see to check the moorings and the cabin locks. You're asking about the little Offshore, now. Mr Mordant's boat. Yes — he took her off on a bit of a cruise, two-three weeks back. One evening it were — but don't ask me when. 'Twas a weekday, that I do remember. He weren't gone above a couple o' days, though. Up the canal he went.'

'Did you see him come back?' asked Quill.

'No, sir. I passed the time o' day with him when he set off, like — but I didn't see him bring the boat back. Must have been late-ish. She weren't there when I took my usual stroll after closing, but I saw her tied up alongside the wharf next morning.'

'Which day was that?'

'Ah, there you've got me, sir. Hold on a minute, though. 'Twas a Thursday. Yes. That's right. We was taking delivery from the brewery — and Thursday's their day. So — let me see — that would mean he set off on the Tuesday evening and came back on the Wednesday night sometime. Like I said, he wasn't away for long.'

'You say he went up the canal,' I said. 'So if he came back and went out into the river, you'd have seen him.'

The innkeeper thought for a moment. 'That don't follow, sir. I've my business to attend to. Mind you — he could only pass through yon lock if the tide was right. Better have a word with the lock-keeper.'

The British Waterways man was definite. Hugo's yacht had not passed through the lock for months. Then how had it reached the North Sea?

'Is there another outlet into the Trent?' I asked. He shook his head.

I glanced along the wharf. The masts of the little vessels swayed gently as a light wind ruffled the water of the basin. By the slipway a scruffy black dog sniffed its way past the upturned dinghies. As I watched idly it selected its target — a trailer used for towing a boat behind a car. With an air of determination, it cocked its leg against one of the trailer's tyres and then trotted away with an expression of smug achievement.

That dog deserved a king-size bone.

I touched Quill's sleeve. 'The trailer,' I said.

We walked across to where the mongrel had left its visiting card.

'I should have thought of this sooner,' I confessed. 'Hugo showed some holiday films only a couple of days before the funeral. I actually saw him launching his boat from this trailer. With one of these things behind his Land Rover he could be at the coast in less than two hours.'

Like a hound on the scent, Quill led the way to where the canal flowed into the basin below a picturesque humped bridge. We trudged along the bank towards Meden Market, less than a mile away, following the course Hugo had taken when he slipped his moorings that Tuesday night. Between the village and the yacht basin stood the ruins of the disused brickyard which flourished in the days when narrow-boats plied the now neglected canal. By the water's edge stood a crumbling wharf and, beside it, a slipway sloped gently into the sluggish current.

A few yards from the canal a roofless

cottage rose from a tangle of weeds where long-dead Victorian length-men once cherished heavily scented roses. To one side of that pathetic ruin stood a large shed with double doors. Within five minutes that shed had yielded its secret. In the thick dust of the floor the narrow tracks of a two-wheeled vehicle were as clear as footprints on the moon. This was where the yacht had stood before that midnight dash to the east coast.

I could picture Hugo's actions so clearly. He must have moved the trailer from the yacht basin earlier in the evening — as soon as he knew that there was a body stowed in the hearse. The Land Rover would have been left at the brickyard, too. Then he would stroll along the canal bank, get the boat ready, and motor along the reed-lined waterway to the old slipway. God knows how long it took him to get the vessel out of the water. The trailer had a winch, and Hugo would have practised the operation thoroughly. Then, the boat hidden in the shed, he would set off in the dusk for that fatal confrontation with Russell Minty.

How had the artist died? By a bullet from that gun which still lay in the pocket of my anorak? No — it lacked a silencer, and any shot would have been heard in the Vicarage next door. On reflection, I decided that Hugo must have run true to form as a crime novelist and settled for that old favourite — the blunt instrument. That must have been difficult. Judging from what Susan had said, Minty had taken my warning to heart. Surely he must have suspected mischief when Hugo came a-roaming in the gloaming. But . . . how much of Susan's story could we believe? I was convinced that she had gone to bring her husband to justice. Dorothy was equally certain that she was his accomplice and had gone with him into hiding. My cousin argued that Hugo could have killed me in his study, yet he had not done so. Why? When he struck that blow Susan had been there — I heard her cry out. What passed between them while I lay unconscious at their feet? How did Susan persuade him to leave me alive?

The manner of Minty's death was a

mystery — and likely to remain so until we caught up with Hugo. What seemed certain was that the painter's body had been carried to the Land Rover, driven to the undertaker's and left in place of poor Mary Porter's mortal remains. Then the old woman's body had been carted out to the Land Rover while the blank windows of those empty houses stared like unseeing eyes on the macabre scene. Within ten minutes Hugo could have been hitching up the trailer and, with luck, he would have been at the coast before two in the morning. Somewhere along that desolate stretch where the flat acres of Lincolnshire meet the sea, Hugo had marked out a slipway which would serve his purpose — one that was usable whatever the state of the tide. Perhaps some memory from his Naval Intelligence days had helped him in his choice. He had a novelist's ability to pigeon-hole facts for future reference.

Then, a straight course due east until the little yacht was hull-down over the horizon. Five or six miles . . . then heave ho! and up she rises . . . the body dragged on deck and pitched overboard before the boat turned westwards again. At that time of year it would be getting light around three. Hugo could be out and back in the daylight before anyone was about. If he'd done his homework thoroughly the tides would have worked for him, saving time and effort. On the way home he must have pulled off the road somewhere in the heart of Lincolnshire, using the boat as a caravan while he ate and caught up on his sleep. Then, in the half-light of a summer's evening, he had returned to the brickyard, launched the boat once more and pottered leisurely down to the yacht basin — a timid ditch-crawler home from an uneventful canal cruise.

But ... how had he explained his absence to Susan? He could only fix the hour of Minty's death after seeing the coffin in the hearse, late on Tuesday evening. Even Hugo's inventive mind must have been strained to concoct a plausible excuse for taking off at such short notice — and so late at night. What had he told her? And had she believed him? Like a spreading stain, suspicion was disfiguring my mental image of Susan. Could Dorothy be right about her? With an accomplice, Hugo's tasks would have been so much easier. But if Susan were involved, she had put on a masterly performance after our dramatic encounter in the early hours. Both Dorothy and I had noticed her unusual composure. Now she had disappeared. It was all a bit beyond me.

Back at the house we found two more police cars on the drive and a bevy of uniformed men searching the premises. Quill held a conference, to which Dorothy and I were not invited, and then came out on to the terrace where we were luxuriating in Hugo's garden chairs and enjoying his gin and orange — the spoils of battle.

'If I were you,' said the Inspector, sinking into a deckchair, 'I'd hie me back to London. The fun's over up here. This is where dull routine starts.'

A uniformed constable stepped on to the terrace and murmured in his ear.

'Damn!' said Quill. He turned to us. 'They've found the Land Rover — in the car park at Manchester Airport. Lord! This complicates matters. I must get over to Maunsley right away.' He stood up. 'I'm leaving a man here. Let him know when you're off. Oh — and don't remove anything from the premises, will you?' He grinned.

'You'll keep in touch?' I asked. He gave a good-natured sigh.

'If I've time. I suppose I owe you that.'

After he had gone I sipped my gin and orange and wondered about Hugo. Manchester Airport. Where would he go at short notice? The holiday season was gathering momentum. Unless he was already booked on a flight, he could only hope for a place on the cancellations list — a chancy business at best. I could not see Hugo, the meticulously careful planner, gnawing his nails in the air terminal lounge and waiting for his name to be called over the P/A system. No — he *must* have booked in advance. Did that explain why my life had been spared? If he had booked on a flight he could not afford to waste time disposing of my lifeless remains. Alive or dead, I was

Hugo's problem, but it seemed he reckoned me less dangerous alive.

I was not flattered.

Encouraged by gin and orange, my mind explored the labyrinth of Hugo's reasoning, where each alternative led to further dividing of the ways. Like Theseus of old, I was groping in the dark. Was the Land Rover a 'plant'? The conclusion — that Hugo had made off by air — was obvious. *Too* obvious?

I could not examine every hypothesis. I must choose one path and follow it to the end, with only the tenuous thread of instinct to guide me.

Spain?

That would be reasonable — at least as a first step. Hugo and Susan were planning to move out there in the autumn, so he probably had funds already transferred to a local bank.

I glanced at my watch. If he had managed an early flight, he could be at the villa already. But where was it? In Spain, Hugo would be in my part of the jungle again. I was as much at home there as in England — and a damned sight more so than ever Hugo would be. For him the prime considerations were low cost of living and less tax paid on his royalties. Wherever he went, the aura of middle-class English superiority at its worst would cling to him. He would demand privilege and servility, slowly becoming a caricature of the Englishman abroad. His last resting place would be an untended grave in an obscure Protestant cemetery. His sort make me writhe with shame in the company of Spanish friends. What more fitting than to end our vendetta in the land I loved?

As a private citizen I enjoyed greater freedom than the police. If I was right about Hugo's destination, this business could be cleared up quickly and quietly.

I set down my empty glass on the table.

'How well do you remember Spain, Dot?'

'Like yesterday, coz. If only we could have those days over again.'

'Maybe we shall. Come into the house. We're going to play a little guessing game.'

10

We watched the film three times, staring intently as Hugo's sun-tanned face grimaced at us from the screen. His lips moved soundlessly, speaking words which had died on the air two years before. There he stood, self-consciously posed before the camera and waving his arms like D. W. Griffith directing a pre-talkie epic. Obedient to his silent command, the camera panned round the crowded beach, the bright colours fading and strengthening as sunlight slashed across the lens. Between the beach and the cluster of sea-front hotels sped a silver express train, its details clearly defined as the moving camera kept pace with the hurtling carriages.

'North of Barcelona,' murmured Dorothy above the whirring of the projector. 'That's the single-track line to Gerona.'

'Turns inland south of Tossa,' I said. 'So that limits the area.'

Back swung the camera to where Hugo gazed seaward through powerful binoculars. Behind him a headland jutted out above a rocky promontory, its brow crowned with a white lighthouse.

'Hold it there!' exclaimed Dorothy, and I pressed the switch to arrest the film with one frame in the gate. 'Now,' she said, 'let's concentrate.'

We stared at the scene, past Hugo's shoulders to the wooded slopes of that hill. Beside the lighthouse a gigantic hoarding advertised CLARKSONS HOLIDAYS. Brightly-coloured frame-tents lay like scattered confetti among the trees. Eighty feet above the sea, a wide road swept round the headland. Beneath that busy highway the railway line disappeared into a tunnel.

'It's no good,' said Dorothy at last. 'It's familiar — and I know we've been there. But it's all so different. Those hotels — they're new. I just can't picture what it was like when we knew it, and that's the only way I'd recognise it properly. Let's see some more.'

On the same reel were shots of busy

streets, crowded with tourists; fishermen mending their nets; and a blurred panorama of the distant beach taken from a leaping speedboat. Then came scenes at the Mordants' villa, with Hugo hectoring a group of patient workmen. With breathless haste the camera swept us back to the coastline for a shot of the lighthouse taken from the far side, where another vast hoarding proclaimed the virtues of CALMAR — whatever that might be. In the final shot, Susan at the wheel of the M.G. sweated in close-up against the background of a white hotel.

'Hold it!' cried Dorothy again. 'That hotel. What's it called?'

The background was slightly out of focus, but the name was clear enough. TERRAMAR.

* ★ *

Next morning, after a decent night's sleep in my own bed, I was ready for the quest. This sort of investigation, not unlike the painstaking research at the museum, was more in my line than the tension and violence of midnight burglary.

The travel agent round the corner was polite but very busy. I was obviously not a potential client, but he was helpful enough to produce an armful of highly-coloured brochures giving full details of 'package holidays' in the sun. I carried them back to the flat and the search began.

Success fell to Dorothy.

'Here we are!' she exclaimed. 'Hotel Terramar . . . Calella de la Costa. We were right. It's north of Barcelona on the Costa Dorada. I remember it now. My hat — how it's changed. Here! D'you realise you can have a fifteen-day holiday for thirty-three guineas? What have I been missing all these years?'

'Never mind the remorse,' I said. 'Let's find the place on a decent map.'

The town — described in the brochure as 'Gateway to the Costa Brava' — lay south of Tossa and Blanes. We must have skirted it dozens of times during child-hood holidays as we travelled down the coast to Barcelona. Somewhere in the hinterland, among the pines and cork trees, lay the villa where — I now felt certain — Hugo had sought refuge.

At mid-day the phone rang. It was Quill.

'Keeping in touch, as promised,' he said. 'Thought you'd like to know that Mrs Mordant has followed her husband's example and shaken the dust of England from her shoes — or, at least, from the tyres of her car. I know . . . I know. Someone has blundered. The car was checked through on a cross-Channel ferry yesterday evening. Some idiot failed to pass our message on to the man on duty. I'll have his guts for garters yet.'

'France?' I asked.

'Le Havre. She was lucky to get the car aboard. It was a last-minute arrangement. Where the devil is she heading?'

I left him to puzzle that one out for himself. I had plans of my own.

At last my roving commission with the museum was to prove useful. In my days as curator I often needed to dash abroad, one jump ahead of professional rivals who could outbid me once an item reached the saleroom. Such frantic flights were occasioned by back-door whispers passed on by Milo Hagerty, and it was Milo — Mr Fixit — who engineered the arrangement with a charter airline so that I could be sure of a seat at the drop of a palimpsest.

I was never sure how he managed it. Nobody seemed to lose on the deal — but that's how it always was with Milo's little schemes. Ask him how it was worth his while and he would murmur something about 'fringe benefits'.

My successor was most accommodating. In the name of the museum, two seats were reserved for Mr Trevithick and Secretary on the afternoon flight to Barcelona. Thank heaven Dorothy's passport was up to date.

We scorched up the M.1 and got to Luton Airport fifteen minutes before take-off. The other passengers had already passed through the departure gate and were walking out towards the BAC 1-11 which gleamed, yellow and silver, in the bright sun.

The hostess brought us afternoon tea over the Pyrenees, and at a few minutes after six we were swinging down in a wide curve above Barcelona. By half past seven we had taken rooms in an hotel at the top of the Ramblas near the Plaza de Cataluña and just a few yards from the Canaletas fountain from which we had drunk as children. Legend maintains that those who taste its waters will never leave Barcelona. Sight of it recalled the far-off moment of disappointment when the family car bore us away — and we knew that the days of magic were full spent and faded.

As we sat in the lounge before dinner I skimmed through *La Vanguardia* while Dorothy studied the fashion pages in *Semana* — just as our parents had done twenty years before. The wheel had turned full circle. It only needed a child to pluck my sleeve and demand attention — then the picture would be complete.

Over our leisurely meal we planned the next move. I had phoned the car-hire people who provide my transport when I'm in Spain. A S.E.A.T. 600 would be at the door by eight o'clock next morning. With luck, we could find the villa before

Susan arrived. She might drive with the devil at her back, but there was a limit to the distance she could cover. Somehow I didn't think she would tackle the Pyrenees at night after a hard day under the blazing sun. If she put up on the French side, she would surely wait until the roads were busy again before crossing the frontier. A solitary M.G. at the Customs barrier in the early morning would be remembered. In a long tourist queue, the same car would pass unnoticed — and that was important to Susan.

Dorothy still had doubts about our enterprise.

'How can you be so sure that Hugo's at the villa?' she asked, reasonably enough.

'I'm not. But it's the best bet. I couldn't stay at home, knowing there was a chance of catching him here.'

'And what happens if you do catch him? Have you thought of that?'

I had. Many times. But I chose not to plan that far ahead. *Sufficient unto the day is the evil thereof.*

★ ★ ★

The new toll-road swept us out by Badalona to where the old highway runs parallel to the coast and the single-track line to Gerona. For some miles we raced alongside a north-bound train, while away to the left the hills closed in until at last we were climbing their lower slopes. For miles my view was limited to the rear of a heavy lorry, its French registration-plate just visible through a cloud of diesel smoke as it pounded towards the border. Every time I eased over to the left, hoping to get past that belching Behemoth, I found the road blocked by oncoming traffic doing a Mille Miglia act astride the white line. I hardly noticed the sea on our right until we rounded a headland beneath a lighthouse, the lorry swung clear of my view, and — for a fleeting moment — Calella lay below us, framed between palm trees and cacti.

The long *playa* stretched into the shimmering distance, its golden sand carpeted with bronzed humanity and the mushroom growth of beach umbrellas. The railway ran through an avenue of palms and on the landward side I glimpsed the flash of glass and chrome as excursion coaches pulled away from the dazzling white hotels in the bright morning sun.

The scene leaped at me for a few seconds, slid sideways along the wind-screen, and vanished as the road carried us half a mile inland. Ten minutes later I was washing the taste of diesel fumes from my mouth as we sipped coffee in a quiet bar off the bustling Calle Iglesia, the main shopping street which runs the length of the old town.

I was anxious to keep my enquiries unofficial. The last thing I wanted was to become involved with the Spanish police. Who could tell how things might turn out? For years I had been an apostle of non-violence, but faced with the prospect of an encounter with Hugo I reacted instinctively. Deep in my unconscious some shaggy prehistoric ancestor was roused from the slumber of centuries. I wondered if Dorothy had noticed how the automatic spoiled the cut of my blazer.

I knew all about automatic weapons — their history and development, calibre, range and efficiency . . . everything except how to use them. I had never fired a shot in my life. The gun in my pocket imparted a sense of power and security. For the first time I understood that dangerous sense of superiority which can be the gunman's undoing. I could calmly contemplate squeezing a trigger. That was almost non-violent. I despised myself — and hated Hugo for dragging me to his level.

In my hotel bedroom in Barcelona I had even practised in front of the wardrobe mirror. But if I used that gun in earnest there could be no question of finesse. To others the skill of the *picador* who wounds but does not kill. A man should know his limitations. I would clamp my left hand round my right wrist, point the gun at the centre of Hugo's chest — the widest part of his body — and gently squeeze the trigger. And if it came to that, I would not want the police remembering inquisitive Señor Trevithick. I must start asking questions somewhere else. The barman directed me to the nearest house-agent.

Outside, the midsummer sun sliced between the roofs, transforming the shops into dark caverns. A cosmopolitan crowd jammed both narrow pavements and overflowed on to the roadway, parting reluctantly as a corrugated Citröen van nosed slowly forward, its engine clattering like a pneumatic drill. In its wake we reached the door of the establishment I sought.

Luck was with us. A silver-haired Don Quixote greeted us with true Spanish courtesy, listened gravely to my story and then informed me that the Señor Mordant I sought had been an honoured client. That was when the villa had been let to tenants while Hugo and Susan were in England. Now the place was converted for permanent residence and had been removed from the books. I wanted my friend's address? But that was the simplest of matters . . .

Within ten minutes we were outside again, armed with full directions for reaching Hugo's hideout.

My eyes still ached from the morning's drive in the dazzling sun, so we equipped ourselves with sunglasses, and, feeling more like a hunter than ever, I lashed out on a pair of 7 × 50 binoculars. Thank heaven currency restrictions were a thing of the past.

We walked to the car along the quieter back streets. Dorothy tapped the leather case which held the binoculars.

'You mean business, Alan. Are you wearing your secret agent's hat today?'

'No. Just taking precautions. If Hugo's at home, I want to see him before he sees me.'

'And then you'll tell the police?'

Though I did not answer, she read my thoughts.

'Extradition? Do we have a treaty with Spain?'

'I'm not waiting to find out. I've come here to get Hugo, and that's just what I'll do — one way or the other.'

I saw her glance sharply at me, but she said nothing more until we reached the car.

The little white S.E.A.T. was an oven. We opened both doors and stood around waiting for the interior to cool. As we lowered ourselves carefully into the seats Dorothy said, 'Whither away, blithe spirit? Do we call on Hugo before lunch?'

I shook my head. 'That's a most uncivilised suggestion. First, we find the villa; then we check if it's occupied. And then . . . '

'Yes?'

The heat had robbed me of all inspiration. 'You tell me,' I said, flatly.

'Then,' she said softly, 'we do the civilised thing and eat. Let's make it a picnic. Hand over some pesetas.'

Clutching a couple of notes, she went off happily in search of food and drink.

It was past mid-day when we saw the villa. It lay below us in a fold of the hills just as we had seen it in Hugo's film. Parking the car off the unmetalled road, we took up a position in the welcome shade of some stunted trees. The house had a deserted air, even when seen through binoculars. The windows were shuttered and the patio was bare — devoid of the furniture and homely muddle which are sure signs of occupation.

Leaving Dorothy busy with cheese and tomatoes, I skirted Hugo's small estate and managed to get within fifty feet of the villa. Beyond that point the trees and shrubs gave way to formal flower beds and well-kept lawns. From the shelter of a dry ditch I raked the house with my glasses. Nothing moved. So ... I had made a mistake. Common sense should have warned me that Hugo was too wily to risk visiting his own villa. One wrong turning in that labyrinth of deduction and here I was, sweating in a Spanish ditch while — for all I knew — Hugo was downing an iced beer in England. A large viridian lizard ventured within a foot of my left shoe and regarded me with profound disgust. I shared his view. I had proved myself a rank amateur.

Then — above the gentle hum of insects — I heard the sound which dispelled gloom and restored my wilting confidence.

Inside that shuttered villa, someone flushed a lavatory.

★ ★ ★

With that prolonged gurgle I was vindicated. As I sat there, listening to the hiss of the refilling cistern, I knew that the villa was occupied by someone anxious to keep his presence secret. No idle tramp would endure the stifling heat of that closed house. Such a scavenger would rifle the larder and then eat in comfort under the open sky.

My elation was short-lived. The next move was up to Hugo. I dared not approach that villa in daylight. Behind those shutters was a desperate man — probably armed. The few pieces of classical statuary in the garden were useless as cover. Until nightfall — in about six hours time — the unseen fugitive had the advantage. There was nothing for it but to wait.

We passed a pleasant afternoon on the hillside above the villa while the wooded ridges further inland tilted inexorably towards the sun. Throughout the whole of that time we saw no movement at the house.

With the brief twilight a cool breeze sighed in from the sea, rustling the leaves over our heads while the cicadas began their twittering background music.

'Time for that social call,' I said, and we set off down the road to the villa. I planned no heroics. This was to be an armed reconnaissance — no more. We were less than half-way to the house when the lights of a car splashed over the crest of the hill behind us. For thirty precious seconds the glare was dissipated among the trees and we had time to hide. Then, with a roar, the car was past us and turning on to the drive leading to the villa. The driver gunned the engine and switched off.

Susan had arrived.

Too late I realised that I should have dealt with Hugo earlier. If Susan was in league with him, the odds against my success had lengthened.

Lights came on in the villa. A good sign. The occupants must feel secure.

'I'd give a lot to know what they're saying,' whispered Dorothy. 'Whose side is she on?'

We had reached the gate at the end of the drive.

'Hang on here,' I said. 'I'll see what I can find out. They've opened the windows. I should be able to hear if I get close enough.'

Avoiding the gravel drive, I crept towards the villa on its blind side, where outbuildings flanked the patio. As I stood in the shadow of the garage another light flashed on behind a small frosted window. The bathroom. I slipped round the patio until I was against the wall of the villa and under that small window. My arrival was heralded by another performance from the lavatory cistern. I waited for the light to go out, but after a couple of minutes I heard the sound of splashing water followed by an ecstatic squeak from Susan.

'*Marvellous!*'

She was in the shower.

An odd one-sided conversation followed. I could hear Susan distinctly as she shouted above the noise of the spray, but the other voice was inaudible. I had to imagine Hugo's part in the dialogue.

'Why not?' Susan's voice was startlingly loud. For a brief moment I had the uncanny sensation that she was speaking for my special benefit — as though she knew I was crouching beneath that window. There was a pause while her question was answered, but she obviously disagreed with the reply.

'Now that *would* be stupid. Anyway, why should they suspect me? I'm supposed to be the injured party, remember. Wait a jiff . . . I'm nearly out.'

A minute later the drumming of the shower died away, and I could hear Susan towelling herself briskly. Then she spoke again.

'Leave it to me. I'll write to Alan Trevithick in the morning. All weepy and remorseful about running out on him the other night.'

This time I could just hear the deeper tone of the other voice, but the words were lost to me. Susan laughed.

'*I'll* convince him,' she said. 'And then he'll pass it on to that Inspector of his. Poor Susan Mordant — all over-wrought. Don't worry. They won't suspect me — and they'll never think of you being here.'

The sound of towelling ceased, and I could hear her moving about the bathroom. Then came the sharp *hiss* of an aerosol spray.

'*Mumble? Mumble?*' Unintelligible questions from the next room.

The spray hissed again.

'We'll cross that bridge when we come to it,' said Susan. 'What we need now is time to think.'

'*Mumble . . . Mumble . . . .Mumble.*'

'Why? Even your best friends wouldn't recognise you in that get-up. There's no sense in staying cooped up here. That *would* look suspicious — and you'd be a bundle of nerves within a week.'

Her words were underlined by another prolonged hiss. Susan took deodorant ads seriously.

'*Mumble.*'

'Oh yes there is. You're driving me to Montserrat tomorrow. I phoned Tony from Toulouse last night. He'll see me at the hospice at one o'clock. He'll know what to do.'

Above me the window went dark and Susan's voice faded to an indistinct murmur. Two minutes later I had rejoined Dorothy.

'Back to the fleshpots of Barcelona,' I whispered.

'You sound pleased with yourself.'

'I am. We can relax for a bit. Susan's fixed an appointment at Montserrat for tomorrow afternoon.'

'The monastery?' I caught the note of surprise in my cousin's voice.

'I know — it sounds a bit out of character, doesn't it? But there you are. I heard it with my own flapping ears. One o'clock at Montserrat — and we couldn't have planned it better ourselves.'

On the journey back to Barcelona I worked out how we should manage things. I knew Montserrat well, chiefly because of Milo Hagerty. Three years before, he had rolled up at my office with a hot tip that the world-famous Jewels of the Madonna were to be disposed of to private buyers. I already knew that the Church authorities planned to sell some of the treasures of Montserrat for the relief of poverty. My information was that they would sell to the Spanish government — on the understanding that the jewels remained on exhibition within the monastery. That seemed an object lesson in how to eat your cake and have it. The only snag was that the government needed time to raise the money. The idea of those jewels being sold privately was fantastic — but Milo had been right too often for me to ignore the rumour.

He was way off course. Still, I spent a pleasant couple of days at the monastery on the strength of his mistake, and that was long enough to learn the geography of the place and something of the daily routine. At one o'clock each day the boy choristers sing in the great church and the place is packed with visitors. Pilgrims are outnumbered by tourists, and any summer's day sees a crowd of thousands. If Susan hoped to be lost in that mass of humanity she was due for disappointment. Only one road enters the monastery and it is possible to check every vehicle as it approaches the end of its long climb from the plain, thousands of feet below. The road snakes upwards, clinging to the edge of the saw-toothed mountain which gives Montserrat its name.

If we climbed that road in the morning, we could await the arrival of Hugo and Susan in their distinctive M.G. Once they left that car the advantage would pass to us. They would hardly risk any fuss in the presence of so many witnesses.

Dorothy — practical as ever — said, 'What do we do when we've got him? You can't chain him up. He may run for it.'

'I doubt that. Where would he run to? Calella is no use now. No — he'll bow to the inevitable. It's best this way. If we'd tackled him at the villa he might have turned nasty. This way we'll manage things in a civilised fashion.'

'*You hope*. How will you get him back to England?'

'Can't say. In any case, it's *them* — not *him*. You were right. Susan's no innocent. I'm just beginning to wonder which of them is the brains of the business. You should have heard her laying down the law to Hugo. It was . . . I don't know . . . *uncanny*. As for getting them back to

England . . . I'll think of something.'

We drove the rest of the way to Barcelona in silence.

★   ★   ★

That night I lay awake trying to make sense of what I had heard at the villa. '*Uncanny*' was no exaggeration for that complete metamorphosis of Susan's character. Until then I had seen her as naïve . . . trusting . . . blind to Hugo's murderous suspicions. What was I to believe now? That she had been party to the scheme which misfired and brought Milo to his untimely grave? But why would Susan want me out of the way? And what about the death of Russell Minty? I had been so sure that the motive behind both murders was Hugo's insane jealousy. But if Susan was his accomplice, that theory broke down.

Had Minty been killed because he knew of the existence of that plot-book? Men have died for less. But why draw attention to his disappearance? Susan's anxiety . . . those hints of an accident

. . . had only served to increase my suspicion of Hugo.

Suddenly, on the threshold of sleep, I stumbled over the truth.

Susan meant me to suspect her husband.

11

'Couldn't we live here? I've fallen in love with the place all over again.'

Dorothy was scattering crumbs to the pigeons as we sat in the Plaza de Cataluña after breakfast next morning. She turned to me hopefully as she spoke.

'What would we use for money?' I asked.

'Surely you could wangle a job. And what about that book you're writing? Authors do earn royalties, don't they?'

I laughed. 'My dear girl, museum appointments aren't just *wangled*. And as for my writing — there's no guarantee that any publisher will even look at it. I'm not Hugo, churning out best-sellers every year.'

At the mention of Hugo she was suddenly grave. 'What will happen to him?' she asked. 'I suppose they're certain to find him guilty.'

I could not answer. Ever since that

sudden flash of intuition during the night I had been staggered by the implications of what I had learned.

'If they do,' continued Dorothy, as though unaware that I had ignored her question, 'I suppose it'll mean a life sentence.'

'You're doing a lot of supposing.'

'A life sentence,' she repeated slowly. 'What will that do to Hugo Mordant? A writer — an intellectual. You can't begin to imagine what it will be like, can you, Alan?'

'It just so happens that I have a very good idea what it's like.'

She caught the bitterness in my tone and grasped my hand impulsively.

'Darling, I'm *sorry*,' she breathed. 'I wasn't thinking. Of course, you'll know only too well.'

Human nature is odd. I'm sure the well-meaning gentry who voted capital punishment off the statute book believed that life imprisonment is a civilised alternative. Yet as I sat there in the sun-scorched Plaza I found myself recalling what life imprisonment actually *is*

— in terms of human suffering. Not for the first time, I questioned the humanity of handing anyone over to such punishment. I once heard someone express surprise that lifers are allowed to furnish their cells with carpets and easy chairs. '*I suppose it's because they're going to be there some time.*' Some time! Fifteen ... twenty ... thirty years. Eighteen months had been enough for me. And they called capital punishment degrading. I would readily have sent Milo Hagerty's killer to the gallows — 'so quick and clean an ending'. But to hand a fellow creature over to the slow degradation with which our legislators have eased their consciences — that was going to be difficult.

I found myself hoping for an excuse to end the wretched affair decently between ourselves — there on Spanish soil. We checked out of the hotel and set off for Montserrat. It was only ten o'clock, and we were well ahead of the main tourist traffic. The sun blazed down and even with both windows open the heat was intense. Twice we were held up where new road-works were under construction.

Without the cooling rush of air through the car, every surface seemed red hot.

Behind her sunglasses Dorothy looked unaffected by the heat.

'I envy Hugo his M.G.,' she said as we began the tortuous climb into the heart of the saw-toothed range. I swung the little car round the first of the hairpin bends.

'I'd value the fresh air,' I said, 'but not the right-hand drive. I wouldn't bring an English car to Spain on principle.'

'Are you serious?'

'Indeed I am. Believe me, the one thing you don't do in this country is get involved in a car accident. It could be difficult for me — and I know the language. But the average phrase-book tourist is at a disadvantage. Disadvantage? He's a non-starter. '*Señale la frase en este libro*' is about as much use as '*The ear-trumpet of my postilion has been struck by lightning*' when you're facing a Spanish court. And the easiest way to find yourself an accident is to forget the rule of the road. In this car the wheel's on the left, so driving on the right becomes natural. *Comprende?*'

Up and up we went, the surrealist peaks towering above us while to the left we looked out over a vast plain, its distant horizon lost in the heat-haze. For much of the way the road was overshadowed by tall trees which cast welcome shade and helped to bring down the temperature inside the car. Then, at last, we emerged from the shadows to see the massive monastic buildings ahead. We parked the car, cooled off with iced coffee in the restaurant, and then strolled a few yards down the road to where we had a clear view of all approaching traffic. The time was half past eleven. An hour later we were still waiting. The road had become busier. A steady stream of tourist coaches disgorged their occupants and roared away down the hill to the coach park.

A quarter to one. Somewhere, a vast tenor bell began tolling, its deep notes echoing round the mountain peaks. For ten minutes I watched the road through the binoculars until my eyes began to ache.

'They're cutting things fine,' murmured Dorothy in my ear — and at that moment

I glimpsed the M.G. racing up through the dappled sunlight beneath the trees, half a mile away.

'Here they come,' I exclaimed triumphantly. We knew what to do. Turning my back on the road, I gazed unseeingly through the binoculars. Dorothy, well disguised by her sunglasses and a straw hat, stood beside me, apparently studying a guide-book but in reality watching that M.G. as though it were a wild animal approaching a trap.

'Who's driving?' I asked, without turning my head.

'Susan. Hugo looks half-asleep. Oh, hell. They're slowing down. There's a jam of coaches up ahead. They're stopping right opposite us. What if we're recognised?'

'Relax. They can't just turn round and go back. The road's too narrow. Get ready to jump on their car if they spot us. Are they looking this way?'

'No. Susan can't see up ahead. This coach is blocking her view. I see what you mean about right-hand drive. Ah — she's asked Hugo to take a look this side. He's getting out. Ha! He's not very pleased with life. Jumpy as a kitten, by the look of him. Now he's getting back in again.'

'How about Susan?' I longed to see for myself if the wild theory I had dreamed up was feasible. A quick glance over my shoulder and I would know the truth — but it was too risky. 'Cool as a cucumber,' said Dorothy. 'Ah, they're moving again.' By way of emphasis, her words were nearly drowned in the roar of engines and a blast of exhaust fumes swept past us. 'Come on,' she added. 'They can't see us now. Let's get up to the car park.'

During our absence the car park had filled up. When it came to leaving, the scriptural principle would hold good and the last would be first. But I had decided that the first would not be last, and had left our car near the entrance. Now, as we came within sight of the parking area, I could see Hugo's green M.G. standing only a few feet from the white S.E.A.T.

I caught Dorothy's hand and we dodged behind an orange and crimson coach from which the heat of the sun radiated like an electric fire. Cautiously, we peered round a corner of the coachwork to where Susan, with her back to us, was leaning over the open two-seater. Her companion had moved into the driving seat, and she seemed to be pointing to something on the floor by his feet. As we watched, he leaned forward to adjust the seat. Susan patted him on the shoulder and walked quickly away towards the monastic buildings.

'What's he going to do?' I muttered. 'Surely he'll not drive off and leave her here?'

'Maybe he's just going to park somewhere else,' said Dorothy.

I stared at the figure in the open car. What had Susan said at the villa? '*Even your best friends wouldn't recognise you in that get-up.*' Certainly no one hunting for Hugo Mordant would look twice at that man. Cropped hair — dark glasses — flowered shirt — all contributed to his disguise. Even I would have been fooled, had I not known his identity.

And now — after all our efforts — we might lose him. I saw the car begin to move slowly forward. A coach-load of tourists wandered in front of it like a flock of sheep. This could be my last chance. Leaving Dorothy staring after me, I sprinted from behind the coach, elbowed my way through the crowd and fetched up beside the M.G. As I placed a hand on its bonnet, the driver looked up, his expression veiled by those dark glasses.

I tried to sound casual.

'*Russell Minty, I presume?*'

★　★　★

I had recognised the artist from our vantage point behind the orange and crimson coach. But then, I was prepared to see him there with Susan. It was the only logical explanation for all that had been happening in the past few weeks. In the night I had turned the matter over and over until the notion that Minty might still be alive became less crazy every time I looked at it.

I'll not deny I felt smug as I stood there, leaning against the little green car and looking down at him. His jaw dropped at the mention of his name. For a moment he seemed frozen in his seat. Then he acted with lightning speed.

His foot came off the clutch pedal, the engine roared, and the car leaped forward. I saw the edge of the wind-shield come at me and threw myself aside, stumbling to one knee. Ahead of the car, the crowd scattered with yells and shrieks.

'Alan! Quick!'

I staggered to my feet to see Dorothy waving to me from beside our car. Within seconds we were off in pursuit.

'He didn't recognise me,' I panted as the needle crept past the fifty mark. 'It's Russell Minty — not Hugo. He'll have a hell of a lot of explaining to do when we catch him.'

Dorothy spared me unnecessary questions. I needed all my mind for driving. The Monte Carlo Rally holds no attractions for me. I'm no competition driver — but at least I was proving better than Russell Minty. His nerves must have been in poor shape. On the right — only a yard from our wheels, the ground fell sheer for hundreds of feet. In the right-hand driving seat of the M.G., Minty must have felt himself hanging over that precipice. He edged the car as far as possible from the verge, until his left-hand wheels were well over the white line down the centre of the road. Within three minutes of leaving the car park we were closing with him. Our speed was way over the safety margin, and Minty was driving recklessly. To attract his attention, I began to sound our horn. I saw him reach up and adjust the driving mirror so that he could see us clearly. As he did so we roared round a bend, and there ahead of us was a silver tourist coach, bouncing and swaying down towards the coach park. With blithe indifference to the rules of the road, the driver kept the huge vehicle astride the white line. Minty's attention had been distracted by his adjustment of the driving mirror and he was going much faster than the coach. His left hand dropped to the steering-wheel again and I knew he was going to overtake. Then — it happened. Faced with the sight of that coach, slap in the middle of the road,

Minty reacted as he would have done on an English highway. He swung the M.G. to the right and began to overtake the coach on its blind side. The driver of the chrome and glass juggernaut probably failed to see the low green sports car when it first flashed into his rear-view mirror. What is certain is that he could not possibly see it once Minty began to overtake on the wrong side. Realising the danger, I sounded my horn again and again. To my horror, the coach driver misunderstood my signal. Thinking I wanted to overtake, he raised his left arm in a nonchalant wave, *and began to pull over to the right to let me pass.*

Even above the roar of the engines I heard Minty's brakes go on as he saw the vast side of the coach closing in on him. The M.G. diced about — its rear end wagging like a rumba dancer's bottom. The coach slid ahead, missing the long green bonnet by inches, but the damage had been done. Another hairpin bend loomed up, and although Minty's speed had dropped to less than thirty his car was out of control. I saw him fighting the wheel as his tyres slid into the dust and loose shale at the very edge of the road. As we drew level, his right-hand front wheel bounced over the primitive kerb of white-painted stones which marked the danger point. Then the front of the car caught the white wooden paling, swinging the rear round towards the precipice. Our own car was swaying alarmingly, and I dared not take my eyes off the road. I heard Dorothy scream, and knew that the M.G. had gone over the edge. As soon as I could I pulled to the side and stopped. The world was very still. The silver coach had disappeared and the road was deserted. Dorothy and I scrambled from the car and ran back along the way we had come.

The history of the tragedy was clearly written on the roadway. Higher up the hill were the black skid marks on the metalled surface. Then came the wide furrows in the dust and the displaced stones. But always the eye was drawn to the shattered fence. By a freak chance three of the uprights remained in position, with fragments of the crossbar still in place.

Silhouetted against the sky they made a strange contemporary Calvary. Beside the central cross we knelt and — leaning cautiously forward — gazed over the edge and down a thousand feet to the treetops below.

12

We drove from the church to the *cementerio* in a sober black car provided by the Consulate. Four of us in air-conditioned sedateness behind an expressionless driver. Dorothy, myself, a diplomatic young man — and Inspector Quill. The diplomatic young man was the most agitated.

'I hope we don't have hysterics at the graveside,' he said, with an accusing glare in Quill's direction. The Inspector leaned back and closed his eyes.

'All will be sweetness and light,' he murmured. 'Mrs Mordant has come to regard me as her father-confessor.'

'I thought that privilege was reserved for Father Whatsit — the priest she was going to see at Montserrat,' said Dorothy. Quill opened one eye. 'The Reverend Anthony Murray,' he said. 'Yes, Miss Merrack, he is by way of being her spiritual adviser, and I must say he advised her very well. When I appeared on the scene yesterday she was ready to unburden her little heart to me. And as soon as this funeral is over she will be equally ready to accompany me to England and answer a few more questions there.'

The man from the Consulate cleared his throat noisily.

'Thank God the authorities are being co-operative,' he muttered. 'This sort of caper can be damned awkward. God knows what might have happened if that M.G. had landed on top of anyone.'

'Your people have put them in the picture,' said Quill serenely. The young man puffed out his cheeks petulantly.

'Well, I wish they'd seen fit to fill me in at the same time,' he complained. 'I've only been given half the story — and that half doesn't make much sense. I thought you were supposed to be looking for Hugo Mordant.'

'Gone! Perished! Scattered to the four winds!' exclaimed Quill in sepulchral tones. 'His too, too solid flesh went up the flue at the Maunsley Crem weeks ago.

Serves him right. That's what he'd planned for Russell Minty.'

I laughed shortly. 'Hugo's clever schemes seemed fated to blow up in his face,' I said. Quill nodded.

'True — but what can you expect from a detective novelist? Unrealistic, the lot of 'em. Too clever by half.'

'He fooled you,' I said hotly. 'And nearly put me away for life. Don't be too superior about his efforts.'

'Point taken,' said Quill affably. 'And, of course, we know how he planned the museum job. It's all in that plot-book. Miss Merrack here was quite right. He was insanely jealous, and the object of the exercise was not Milo Hagerty's death, but yours. So he still had a score to settle with you. But in the meantime Russell Minty had loomed over his domestic horizon and — he was convinced — seduced his wife. What a suspicious mind that man had!'

'Not without cause,' said Dorothy, quietly. 'Susan Mordant is a silly little fool. D'you mean to tell me she didn't know her husband was being tormented out of his mind by what she was doing? Surely she noticed *something*. And to start those clandestine visits to Russell Minty when she knew how people had misunderstood her visits to Alan two years before . . . well . . . that was asking for trouble.'

'Ah,' said Quill profoundly. 'But there was a difference. She and Minty were lovers.'

'Good Lord!' exclaimed the diplomat. 'So it was the old eternal triangle. And the wretched husband got himself clobbered. Sort of poetic justice, what?'

Quill shook his head. 'It wasn't quite so simple. Hugo Mordant suspected Minty of having an affair with his wife — so he planned the perfect murder, or so he fondly imagined. He'd found out that the local undertaker often left the odd corpse lying about in the bottom of his hearse. Complete with coffin, of course. So he planned to murder Minty, substitute his body for one thoughtfully provided by the undertaker, and then ditch the spare body out at sea. If it ever bobbed to the surface, no one would link it with Russell

Minty and, if Hugo Mordant played his cards carefully, no one would ever associate him with this disappearance of the artist.'

'What exactly did go wrong?' asked Dorothy. Quill glanced round the eager faces of the group.

'I suppose you deserve to know,' he said quietly. 'Well, Hugo Mordant's trouble was that his sense of the dramatic was over-developed. He confronted Minty with a silenced automatic and then — knowing he had him at his mercy — proceeded to boast about what he was going to do. He told Minty how he had rehearsed his plan time and again. He explained all about the body in the hearse, and how he had already moved the yacht, on its trailer, to the brickyard. He even told him the launching site he'd picked on the Lincolnshire coast. My word, he must have been pleased with his little self.'

'But Minty should have been on his guard,' I exclaimed. 'I *warned* him.'

Quill raised a calming hand. 'And not in vain. Minty told Mrs Mordant of your visit and they manned the barricades. The only snag was, they had to wait for friend Hugo to move first. They couldn't very well clobber him without reason — and Mordant made damn sure he gave them none. Of course Minty was suspicious when Mordant called late that evening. But what could he do? On the surface they were supposed to be good neighbours. He could hardly slam the door in his face. So he invited him in — and it was only when they were having drinks in the lounge that Mordant produced his artillery and proceeded to inform Minty of the fate that awaited him. But . . . '

The Inspector paused dramatically and grinned at our obvious excitement.

' . . . But relief was at hand. The Seventh Cavalry, in the form of Mrs Mordant, was about to appear on the scene. When Minty saw Mordant drive up in his Land Rover, he telephoned Mrs Mordant before he opened his front door. She arrived a few minutes later, let herself in quietly and, at the crucial moment, burst into the lounge. In the general scrimmage that followed, Minty felled

Mordant with a swipe from a poker and then proceeded to hammer home a few more blows before it dawned on his consciousness that the wretched fellow had breathed his last. An untoward complication.'

'Self-defence.' My sympathies were all with Minty. Quill glared at me.

'What's that supposed to mean?' he growled. 'It's no magic formula, y'know. It doesn't give you the right to kill someone who's threatening you.'

'Not even if they have a silenced automatic?' I queried.

'Not even then,' he replied, seriously. 'And don't forget, what I'm telling you is only what Mrs Mordant told me. Unsubstantiated evidence. Still — it's all we can hope for now, I suppose. Anyway — there was Mordant, stiffening on the hearth-rug. Things looked bleak for our star-crossed lovers.' He turned to the young man from the Consulate. 'You said it was the eternal triangle. Well, that's just how it would have looked if we'd been called in at that moment. Dead husband, unfaithful wife — and lover clutching blood-stained poker. From what I gather, Minty was badly shaken. It was Mrs Mordant who had the idea of using her husband's carefully prepared plan to dispose of his body — and that's just what they did. They wrapped the body in Minty's old duffle coat, lugged it out to the Land Rover, and drove to the street behind the undertaker's place. Then they switched the bodies, drove to the brick-yard, hitched on the trailer and made for the coast. Minty had handled that yacht before — as you'll have gathered from those holiday films — and, for good measure, he was in Air-Sea Rescue for a time. So the trip out to sea presented no difficulties.'

I glanced at the road ahead, where a flamboyant hearse was bearing Minty's body on its last journey.

'Didn't they have any scruples about ditching poor old Mary Porter's body?' I asked.

Quill shrugged his shoulders. 'Maybe. Minty was a sensitive man. But the alternative looked like being a life-time in prison — and you'd already convinced him how undesirable *that* was. They must have weighted the body in an amateurish fashion. That's how it came to break loose so soon. Then they sneaked back to Meden Market. In the meantime Mordant's body had been disposed of — thanks to that undertaker, the Vicar and the crematorium staff.'

'And Minty went into hiding,' said Dorothy. 'Where?'

Quill leaned back and — to my surprise — produced a snuff-box from his pocket.

'He moved around a bit,' he said, helping himself to a liberal pinch and dusting the front of his jacket with a large khaki handkerchief. 'Part of the time he was living with Mrs Mordant at her home. Keeping out of sight, of course. Then for a while he stayed in London — in an hotel off the King's Road.'

'Was that where he phoned from when Dorothy and I visited Susan on the way back from York?' I asked. Quill nodded.

'I gather he took you in nicely. But then, he was something of a mimic, by all accounts.'

I remembered Minty's brilliant impersonation of a village copper.

'I didn't suspect a thing. But I thought there was some dirty work a-brewing when he suggested dinner at my flat.'

Quill blew his nose noisily. 'Ironic,' he boomed from behind his handkerchief. 'Minty really did want to meet you. He was quite sincere about coming to your flat for dinner. You see, he believed you were the only person who could help him. After all, you had been the victim of a miscarriage of justice, so he felt sure you'd understand his position. But, of course, he couldn't say all that over the phone.'

'And I put him off.' Overwhelming compassion for the artist assailed me. All my good intentions had only compassed his destruction. My impetuosity had raised the curtain on that final tragic act, and my urgent blasts on the horn had summoned death with a royal fanfare to the Montserrat road.

Quill looked at me sympathetically, as though reading my thoughts.

'You weren't to know,' he said. 'In a

sense, he was hoist with his own petard. He had to create the illusion that Hugo Mordant was still alive, and he was so convincing that you instinctively mistrusted him.'

'I still don't see how they hoped to get away with it,' said Dorothy. 'Sooner or later somebody would start wondering about Hugo and asking where he was. What then?'

The Inspector beamed at her. 'You're quite right, Miss Merrack. But, you see, Mrs Mordant was going to start the questions herself. The plan was quite simple. Minty was to come over to Spain and lie low for a bit. Then, as soon as he was out of the way, she was to start getting anxious about her absent husband. Eventually she would call us in and when we searched the house for a lead to his disappearance, there would be that plot-book — slap bang in the middle of his desk. Meden Market was already twittering because our chaps were asking questions about Mary Porter's funeral, so it was obvious we were on to something. By spoon-feeding us that plot-book, Mrs

Mordant hoped to convince us that Minty was dead and Hugo Mordant a murderer on the run. Mr Trevithick here would support that idea. He had told Minty his suspicions, and they knew that he'd already seen the plot-book.'

'Susan had got me weighed up all right,' I said ruefully, remembering what I had overheard at the villa. Quill nodded.

'We had nothing on her. After a few months she would have come out to Spain and settled at the villa. It belonged to her, together with a number of assets Mordant had made over, to avoid tax. Then Minty would join her and they'd live happily ever after.' He turned to me. 'When you burgled the house that night you upset their timetable. Minty was to set off in a matter of hours. He mistook you for a common-or-garden villain and flattened you before Mrs Mordant pointed out his mistake. He couldn't be certain if you'd recognised him, and he wasn't going to hang around to find out. As soon as she realised that you still believed Minty to be dead, Mrs Mordant set off for Spain — to put her lover's mind at rest and to salvage what she could of their scheme. They might have pulled it off, if you hadn't been so set on a vendetta with Hugo Mordant.'

I grinned. 'Are you trying to tell us that amateur interference has its uses?'

He did not reply. Instead he said, 'What made you suspect that Minty was still alive?'

'It was a muddled sort of process. I was more than half-asleep and my thoughts were running wild. What I'd overheard at the villa had given me new insight into Susan's character. There was depth there. I hadn't been taking her seriously enough. Then I thought of what she'd told me about Hugo. She'd been planting suspicion in my mind. *Why?* If she wanted him arrested, she should have told her suspicions to your people. If she didn't want that — what *did* she want? What use was my suspicion? Then I got to thinking about Hugo — and it dawned on me that I hadn't seen him since that weekend when he tried to shove me off the church tower. The significance of that didn't register at first. After all — I'd *heard* him. On the phone and at the villa. But had I? Looking back, I realised that the voice on the phone was distorted, while the man at the villa was almost inaudible. It could have been anyone. I assumed it was Hugo — and Susan had fostered that idea. Why had I accepted that distorted voice on the phone as being Hugo's? Because Susan had told me that he was calling me from London. But what about that encounter in the small hours of the morning? I had been too dazzled by the fluorescent light to identify my assailant — but Dorothy had seen him as he dashed for the Land Rover, just as she had seen him later on the Montserrat road. And on both occasions she had spoken of him as Hugo. It had not occurred to me that she wouldn't know Hugo from Adam. She had simply assumed that the man who turned up where Hugo was expected to be, must be Hugo. And on that first occasion Susan had not corrected her. Now, if it wasn't Hugo — *who was it?* That's when I had the crazy idea about Russell Minty. It was completely cockeyed — yet it made sense of everything. If Minty was alive, it could only mean that Hugo was dead — and if Susan wanted to keep his death a secret, what better way than by creating the illusion that he was still alive? Of course, Hugo could never appear, but if we believed he was a murderer on the run, we wouldn't expect an appearance. You're right. It could have worked. Specially as we'd convinced ourselves that Russell Minty was dead.' I raised an eyebrow at Dorothy.

'Hold hard. Hold hard,' exclaimed the diplomat. 'If Russell Minty was officially dead, he couldn't very well come back to life again. What about his passport? If he wanted to live in Spain he'd have to go through a lot of legal rigmarole. Someone would be bound to spot his name — specially if the case had got into the papers.'

Quill shook his head. 'I'd agree with all that if we were talking about Hugo Mordant. But Russell Minty was a very different creature. He cared nothing for property and legal fal-lal. His chief asset lay in his art, and once he'd left England he would happily wave goodbye to whatever little he possessed there, including his name.'

'Huh?' Dorothy spoke for the rest of us.

The Inspector looked a shade embarrassed. 'All right — I might as well admit that this was news to me and we might never have guessed it,' he said. 'The fact is . . . '*Russell Minty*' wasn't his real name at all. He adopted it years ago — just after the war when he began to study art seriously. And he used it all the time except on his passport, where the details had to tally with those on his birth certificate.'

'It sounds highly suspicious to me,' said the diplomat.

'Using a false name. Most reprehensible. I could understand it if he'd been a writer. *Nom de plume* and all that, y'know. But a *painter* . . . .Can't see the point at all.'

'You will, Oscar. You will,' murmured Quill. He reached into his pocket and produced a British passport. 'There you are,' he said, tossing it into my lap. 'Russell Minty's dreadful secret.'

I gazed at the picture of the bearded artist. It was a good likeness. That was how I wanted to remember him — not as the terrified fugitive in the M.G., and certainly not as the shattered corpse I had to identify after the accident.

I turned back one page and understood . . .

Poor devil! What budding artist could stand being lumbered with a name like that?

Edmund Landseer.

Quill caught my eye. 'Yes,' he said. '*The Monarch of the Glen* would have been a heavy weight round his neck. He's being buried as Russell Minty. One day we may be proud to have known him.'

★   ★   ★

As we moved away from the open grave I saw Quill lay a hand gently on Susan Mordant's arm. He could have been expressing sincere condolences. She nodded slowly, and side by side they walked to a waiting car. I could well imagine what he was saying. He had said it all to me, once.

'Is he just going to ask her more questions?' asked Dorothy as we stood watching the car dwindle down the dusty road.

I knew my Quill better than that. Three men had died. Society would expect some payment on account.

'As soon as they reach England he'll arrest her as being accessory to the murder of Hugo Mordant,' I said. 'And it's no use looking shocked. It's his job. He does it rather well. We should just be back from our honeymoon in time to give evidence. God! What a prospect!'

'But they'll let her off, won't they?'

Twelve good men and true?

'Don't bet on it,' I said.

THE END